JEFF BROWN

FLAT STANLEY
and Other Adventures

Flat Stanley
Stanley and the Magic Lamp
Stanley in Space

Mammoth

FLAT STANLEY

Illustrated by Tomi Ungerer

For J.C. and Tony

Breakfast was ready.

'I will go and wake the boys,' Mrs Lambchop said to her husband, George Lambchop. Just then their younger son, Arthur, called from the bedroom he shared with his brother Stanley in their New York home.

'Hey! Come and look! Hey!'

Mr and Mrs Lambchop were both very much in favour of politeness and careful speech. 'Hay is for horses, Arthur, not people,' Mr Lambchop said as they entered the bedroom. 'Try to remember that.'

'Excuse me,' Arthur said. 'But look!'

He pointed to Stanley's bed. Across it lay the enormous bulletin board that Mr Lambchop had given the boys a Christmas ago, so that they could pin up pictures and messages and maps. It had fallen, during the night, on top of Stanley.

But Stanley was not hurt. In fact he would still have been sleeping if he had not been woken by his brother's shout.

'What's going on here?' he called out cheerfully from beneath the enormous board.

Mr and Mrs Lambchop hurried to lift it from the bed.

'Heavens!' said Mrs Lambchop

'Gosh!' said Arthur. 'Stanley's flat!'

'As a pancake,' said Mr Lambchop. 'Darndest thing I've ever seen.'

'Let's all have breakfast,' Mrs Lambchop said. 'Then Stanley and I will go and see Doctor Dan and hear what he has to say.'

The examination was almost over.

'How do you feel?' Doctor Dan asked. 'Does it hurt very much?'

'I felt sort of tickly for a while after I got up,' Stanley Lambchop said, 'but I feel fine now.'

'Well, that's mostly how it is with these cases,' said Doctor Dan.

'We'll just have to keep an eye on this young fellow,' he said when he had finished the examination. 'Sometimes we doctors, despite all our years of training and experience, can only marvel at how little we really know.'

Mrs Lambchop said she thought that Stanley's clothes would have to be altered by the tailor now, so Doctor Dan told his nurse to take Stanley's measurements.

EYE

Mrs Lambchop wrote them down.

Stanley was four feet tall, about a foot wide, and half an inch thick.

When Stanley got used to being flat, he enjoyed it.

He could go in and out of rooms, even when the door was closed, just by lying down and sliding through the crack at the bottom.

Mr and Mrs Lambchop said it was silly, but they were quite proud of him.

Arthur got jealous and tried to slide under a door, but he just banged his head.

Being flat could also be helpful, Stanley found.

He was taking a walk with Mrs Lambchop one afternoon when her favourite ring fell from her finger. The ring rolled

across the pavement and down between
the bars of a grating that covered a dark,
deep shaft. Mrs Lambchop began to cry.

'I have an idea,' Stanley said.

He took the laces out of his shoes and

an extra pair out of his pocket and tied
them all together to make one long lace.
Then he tied the end of that to the back
of his belt and gave the other end to his
mother.

'Lower me,' he said, 'and I will look
for the ring.'

'Thank you, Stanley,' Mrs Lambchop
said. She lowered him between the bars
and moved him carefully up and down
and from side to side, so that he could

search the whole floor of the shaft.

Two policemen came by and stared at Mrs Lambchop as she stood holding the long lace that ran down through the grating. She pretended not to notice them.

'What's the matter, lady?' the first policeman asked. 'Is your yo-yo stuck?'

'I am not playing with a yo-yo!' Mrs Lambchop said sharply. 'My son is at the other end of this lace, if you must know.'

'Humour her, Harry,' said the second policeman. 'The poor soul's dotty as can be!'

Just then, down in the shaft, Stanley cried out, 'Horray!'

Mrs Lambchop pulled him up and saw that he had the ring.

'Good for you, Stanley,' she said. Then she turned angrily to the policemen.

'Dotty, indeed!' she said. 'Shame!'

The policemen apologized. 'We didn't get it, lady,' they said. 'We have been hasty. We see that now.'

'People should think twice before making rude remarks,' said Mrs Lambchop. 'And then not make them at all.'

The policemen realized that was a good rule and said they would try to remember it.

One day Stanley got a letter from his friend Thomas Anthony Jeffrey, whose family had moved recently to California. A school holiday was about to begin and Stanley was invited to spend it with the Jeffreys.

'Oh, boy!' Stanley said. 'I would love to go!'

Mr Lambchop sighed. 'A round trip or aeroplane ticket to California is very expensive,' he said. 'I shall have to think of some cheaper way.'

When Mr Lambchop came home from the office that evening, he brought with him an enormous brown-paper envelope.

'Now then, Stanley,' he said. 'Try this for size.'

The envelope fitted Stanley very well. There was even room left over, Mrs

Lambchop discovered, for an egg-salad sandwich made with thin bread, and a flat cigarette case filled with milk.

They had to put a great many stamps on the envelope to pay for both airmail and insurance, but it was still much less expensive than a train or aeroplane ticket to California would have been.

The next day Mr and Mrs Lambchop slid Stanley into his envelope, along with the egg-salad sandwich and the cigarette case full of milk, and mailed him from the box on the corner. The envelope had to be folded to fit through the slot, but Stanley was a limber boy and inside the box he straightened up again.

Mrs Lambchop was nervous because Stanley had never been away from home alone before. She rapped on the box.

'Can you hear me, dear?' she called.
'Are you all right?'

Stanley's voice came quite clearly. 'I'm
fine. Can I eat my sandwich now?'

'Wait an hour. And try not to get overheated, dear,' Mrs Lambchop said. Then she and Mr Lambchop cried out 'Good-bye, good-bye!' and went home.

Stanley had a fine time in California. When the visit was over, the Jeffreys returned him in a beautiful white envelope they had made themselves. It had red-and-blue markings to show that it was airmail, and Thomas Jeffrey had lettered it 'Valuable' and 'Fragile' and 'This End Up' on both sides.

Back home Stanley told his family that he had been handled so carefully he never felt a single bump. Mr Lambchop said it proved that jet planes were wonderful, and so was the Post Office Department, and that this was a great age in which to live.

Stanley thought so too.

Mr Lambchop had always liked to take the boys off with him on Sunday afternoons to a museum or roller-skating in the park, but it was difficult when they were crossing streets or moving about in crowds. Stanley and Arthur would often be jostled from his side and Mr Lambchop worried about speeding taxis or that hurrying people might accidentally knock them down.

It was easier after Stanley got flat.

Mr Lambchop discovered that he could roll Stanley up without hurting him at all. He would tie a piece of string around Stanley to keep him from unrolling and make a little loop in the string for himself. It was as simple as carrying a parcel, and he could hold on to Arthur with the other hand.

Stanley did not mind being carried because he had never much liked to walk. Arthur didn't like walking either, but he had to. It made him mad.

One Sunday afternoon, in the street, they met an old college friend of Mr Lambchop's, a man he had not seen for years.

'Well, George, I see you have bought some wallpaper,' the man said. 'Going to decorate your house, I suppose?'

'Wallpaper?' said Mr Lambchop. 'Oh, no. This is my son Stanley.'

He undid the string and Stanley unrolled.

'How do you do?' Stanley said.

'Nice to meet you, young feller,' the man said. He said to Mr Lambchop, 'George, that boy is flat.'

'Smart, too,' Mr Lambchop said. 'Stanley is third from the top in his class at school.'

'Phooey!' said Arthur.

'This is my younger son, Arthur,' Mr Lambchop said. 'And he will apologize for his rudeness.'

Arthur could only blush and apologize.

Mr Lambchop rolled Stanley up again and they set out for home. It rained quite hard while they were on the way. Stanley, of course, hardly got wet at all, just around the edges, but Arthur got soaked.

Late that night Mr and Mrs Lambchop heard a noise out in the living room. They found Arthur lying on the floor near the bookcase. He had piled a great many volumes of the *Encyclopaedia Britannica* on top of himself.

'Put some more on me,' Arthur said when he saw them. 'Don't just stand there. Help me.'

Mr and Mrs Lambchop sent him back to bed, but the next morning they spoke to Stanley. 'Arthur can't help being jealous,' they said. 'Be nice to him. You're his big brother, after all.'

Stanley and Arthur were in the park. The day was sunny, but windy too, and many older boys were flying beautiful, enormous kites with long tails, made in all the colours of the rainbow.

Arthur sighed. 'Some day,' he said, 'I will have a big kite and I will win a kite-

flying contest and be famous like everyone else. *Nobody* knows who I am these
days.'

Stanley remembered what his parents
had said. He went to a boy whose kite
was broken and borrowed a large spool
of string.

'You can fly me, Arthur,' he said.
'Come on.'

He attached the string to himself and
gave Arthur the spool to hold. He ran
lightly across the grass, sideways to get
up speed, and then he turned to meet the
breeze.

Up, up, up . . . UP! went Stanley,
being a kite.

He knew just how to manage on the
gusts of wind. He faced full into the wind
if he wanted to rise, and let it take him

from behind when he
wanted speed. He had
only to turn his
thin edge to the wind,
carefully, a little
at a time, so that
it did not hold him,
and then he would slip
gracefully down towards
the earth again.

Arthur let out all the string and Stanley soared high above the trees, a beautiful sight in his pale sweater and bright brown trousers, against the pale-blue sky.

Everyone in the park stood still to watch.

Stanley swooped right and then left in long, matched swoops. He held his arms by his sides and zoomed at the ground like a rocket and curved up again towards the sun. He sideslipped and circled, and made figure eights and crosses and a star.

Nobody has ever flown the way Stanley Lambchop flew that day. Probably no one ever will again.

After a while, of course, people grew tired of watching and Arthur got tired of running about with the empty spool.

Stanley went right on though, showing off.

Three boys came up to Arthur and invited him to join them for a hot dog and some soda pop. Arthur left the spool wedged in the fork of a tree. He did not notice, while he was eating the hot dog, that the wind was blowing the string and tangling it about the tree.

The string got shorter and shorter, but Stanley did not realize how low he was until leaves brushed his feet, and then it was too late. He got stuck in the branches. Fifteen minutes passed before Arthur and the other boys heard his cries and climbed up to set him free.

Stanley would not speak to his brother that evening, and at bedtime, even though Arthur had apologized, he was still cross.

Alone with Mr Lambchop in the living room, Mrs Lambchop sighed and shook her head. 'You're at the office all day, having fun,' she said. 'You don't realize what I go through with the boys. They're very difficult.'

'Kids are like that,' Mr Lambchop said. 'Phases. Be patient, dear.'

Mr and Mrs O. Jay Dart lived in the flat just above the Lambchops. Mr Dart was an important man, the director of a Famous Museum of Art in the city.

Stanley Lambchop had noticed in the lift that Mr Dart, who was ordinarily a cheerful man, had become quite gloomy, but he had no idea what the reason was. And then at breakfast one morning he heard Mr and Mrs Lambchop talking about Mr Dart.

'I see,' said Mr Lambchop, reading the paper over his coffee cup, 'that yet another painting has been stolen from the Famous Museum. A Toulouse-Lautrec.'

Mrs Lambchop sipped her coffee. 'That probably made it easy to steal,' she said. 'Being too loose, I mean.'

'It says,' Mr Lambchop went on, 'that Mr O. Jay Dart, the director, is at his wits' end. The police are no help. Listen to what the Chief of Police told the newspaper. "We suspect a gang of sneak thieves. These are the worst kind. They work by sneakery, which makes them very difficult to catch. However, my men and I will keep trying. Meanwhile, I hope people will buy tickets for the Policemen's Ball and not park their cars where signs say don't." '

The next morning Stanley Lambchop heard Mr Dart talking to his wife in the lift.

'These sneak thieves work at night,' Mr Dart said. 'It is very hard for our guards to stay awake when they have been on duty all day. And the Famous Museum is so big we cannot guard every picture at the same time. I fear it is hopeless, hopeless, hopeless!'

Suddenly, as if an electric light bulb had lit up in the air above his head, giving out little shooting lines of excitement, Stanley Lambchop had an idea. He told it to Mr Dart.

'Stanley,' Mr Dart said, 'if your mother will give her permission, I will put you and your plan to work this very night!'

Mrs Lambchop gave her permission. 'But you will have to take a long nap this afternoon,' she said. 'I won't have you up till all hours unless you do.'

That evening, after a long nap, Stanley went with Mr Dart to the Famous Museum. Mr Dart took him into the main hall, where the biggest and most important paintings were hung. He pointed to a huge painting that showed a bearded man, wearing a floppy velvet hat, playing a violin for a lady who lay on a couch. There was a half-man, half-horse person standing behind them, and three fat children with wings were flying around above. That, Mr Dart explained,

was the most expensive painting in the world!

There was an empty picture frame on the opposite wall. We shall hear more about that later on.

Mr Dart took Stanley into his office and said, 'It is time for you to put on a disguise.'

'I had already thought of that,' Stanley Lambchop said, 'and I brought one. My cowboy suit. It has a red bandanna that I can tie over my face. Nobody will recognize me in a million years.'

'No,' Mr Dart said. 'You will have to wear the disguise I have chosen.'

From a closet he took a white dress with a blue sash, a pair of shiny little pointed shoes, a wide straw hat with a blue band that matched the sash, and a

wig and a stick.

The wig was made of blond hair, long and done in ringlets. The stick was curved at the top and it, too, had a blue ribbon on it.

'In this shepherdess disguise,' Mr Dart said, 'you will look like a painting that belongs in the main hall. We do not have cowboy pictures in the main hall.'

Stanley was so disgusted that he could hardly speak. 'I shall look like a girl, that's what I shall look like,' he said. 'I wish I had never had my idea.'

But he was a good sport, so he put on the disguise.

Back in the main hall Mr Dart helped Stanley climb up into the empty picture frame. Stanley was able to stay in place because Mr Dart had cleverly put four small spikes in the wall, one for each hand and foot.

The frame was a perfect fit. Against the wall, Stanley looked just like a picture.

'Except for one thing,' Mr Dart said. 'Shepherdesses are supposed to look happy. They smile at their sheep and at the sky. You look fierce, not happy, Stanley.'

Stanley tried hard to get a faraway look in his eyes and even to smile a little bit.

Mr Dart stood back a few feet and stared at him for a moment. 'Well,' he said, 'it may not be art, but I know what I like.'

He went off to make sure that certain other parts of Stanley's plan were being taken care of, and Stanley was left alone.

It was very dark in the main hall. A

little bit of moonlight came through the windows, and Stanley could just make out the world's most expensive painting on the opposite wall. He felt as though the bearded man with the violin and the lady on the couch and the half-horse person and the winged children were all waiting, as he was, for something to happen.

Time passed and he got tireder and tireder. Anyone would be tired this late at night, especially if he had to stand in a picture frame balancing on little spikes.

Maybe they won't come, Stanley thought. Maybe the sneak thieves won't come at all.

The moon went behind a cloud and then the main hall was pitch dark. It seemed to get quieter, too, with the darkness. There was absolutely no sound at all. Stanley felt the hair on the back of his neck prickle beneath the golden curls of the wig.

Cr-eee-eee-k . . . .

The creaking sound came from right out in the middle of the main hall and even as he heard it Stanley saw, in the same place, a tiny yellow glow of light!

The creaking came again and the glow got bigger. A trap door had opened in the floor and two men came up through it into the hall!

Stanley understood everything all at once. These must be the sneak thieves! They had a secret trap door entrance into the museum from outside. That was why they had never been caught. And now, tonight, they were back to steal the most expensive painting in the world!

He kept very still in his picture frame and listened to the sneak thieves.

'This is it, Max,' said the first one. 'This is where we art robbers pull a sensational job whilst the civilized community sleeps.'

'Right, Luther,' said the other man. 'In all this great city there is no one to suspect us.'

Ha, ha! thought Stanley Lambchop. That's what you think!

The sneak thieves put down their lantern and took the world's most expensive painting off the wall.

'What would we do to anyone who tried to capture us, Max?' the first man asked.

'We would kill him. What else?' his friend replied.

That was enough to frighten Stanley, and he was even more frightened when Luther came over and stared at him.

'This sheep girl,' Luther said. 'I

thought sheep girls were supposed to smile, Max. This one looks scared.'

Just in time, Stanley managed to get a faraway look in his eyes again and to smile, sort of.

'You're crazy, Luther,' Max said. 'She's smiling. And what a pretty little thing she is, too.'

That made Stanley furious. He waited until the sneak thieves had turned back to the world's most expensive painting, and then he shouted in his loudest, most terrifying voice: 'POLICE! POLICE! MR DART! THE SNEAK THIEVES ARE HERE!'

The sneak thieves looked at each other. 'Max,' said the first one, very quietly, 'I think I heard the sheep girl yell.'

'I think I did too,' said Max in a quivery

voice. 'Oh, boy! Yelling pictures. We
both need a rest.'

'You'll get a rest, all right!' shouted
Mr Dart, rushing in with the Chief of
Police and lots of guards and policemen

behind him. 'You'll get *ar-rested*, that's what! Ha, ha, ha!'

The sneak thieves were too mixed up by Mr Dart's joke and too frightened by the policemen to put up a fight. Before they knew it, they had been handcuffed and led away to jail.

The next morning in the office of the Chief of Police Stanley Lambchop got a medal. The day after that his picture was in all the newspapers.

For a while Stanley Lambchop was a famous name. Everywhere that Stanley went, people stared and pointed at him. He could hear them whisper, 'Over there, Harriet, over there! That must be Stanley Lambchop, the one who caught the sneak thieves . . .' and things like that.

But after a few weeks the whispering

FLAT HERO

and the staring stopped. People had other things to think about. Stanley did not mind. Being famous had been fun, but enough was enough.

And then came a further change, and it was not a pleasant one. People began to laugh and make fun of him as he passed by. 'Hello, Super-Skinny!' they would shout, and even ruder things, about the way he looked.

Stanley told his parents how he felt. 'It's the other kids I mostly mind,' he said. 'They don't like me any more because I'm different. Flat.'

'Shame on them,' Mrs Lambchop said. 'It is wrong to dislike people for their shapes. Or their religion, for that matter, or the colour of their skin.'

'I know,' Stanley said. 'Only maybe it's impossible for everybody to like *everybody*.'

'Perhaps,' said Mrs Lambchop. 'But they can try.'

Later that night Arthur Lambchop was woken by the sound of crying. In the

darkness he crept across the room and knelt by Stanley's bed.

'Are you okay?' he said.

'Go away,' Stanley said.

'Don't be mad at me,' Arthur said. 'You're still mad because I let you get tangled the day you were my kite, I guess.'

'Skip it, will you?' Stanley said. 'I'm not mad. Go away.'

'Please let's be friends. . . .' Arthur couldn't help crying a little, too. 'Oh, Stanley,' he said. 'Please tell me what's wrong?'

Stanley waited for a long time before he spoke. 'The thing is,' he said, 'I'm just not happy any more. I'm tired of being flat. I want to be a proper shape again, like other people. But I'll have to go on being flat for ever. It makes me sick.'

'Oh, Stanley,' Arthur said. He dried his tears on a corner of Stanley's sheet and could think of nothing more to say.

'Don't talk about what I just said,'

Stanley told him. 'I don't want the folks to worry. That would only make it worse.'

'You're brave,' Arthur said. 'You really are.'

He took hold of Stanley's hand. The two brothers sat together in the darkness, being friends. They were both still sad, but each one felt a *little* better than he had before.

And then, suddenly, though he was not even trying to think, Arthur had an idea. He jumped up and turned on the light and ran to the big storage box where toys and things were kept. He began to rummage in the box.

Stanley sat up in bed to watch.

Arthur flung aside a football and some lead soldiers and aeroplane models and lots of wooden blocks, and then he said,

'Aha!' He had found what he wanted—
an old bicycle pump. He held it up, and
Stanley and he looked at each other.

'Okay,' Stanley said at last. 'But take
it easy.' He put the end of the long pump
hose in his mouth and clamped his lips

tightly about it so that no air could escape.

'I'll go slowly,' Arthur said. 'If it hurts or anything, wiggle your hand at me.'

He began to pump. At first nothing happened except that Stanley's cheeks bulged a bit. Arthur watched his hand, but there was no wiggle signal, so he pumped on. Then, suddenly, Stanley's top half began to swell.

'It's working! It's working!' shouted Arthur, pumping away.

Stanley spread his arms so that the air could get round inside him more easily. He got bigger and bigger. The buttons of his pyjama top burst off—*Pop! Pop! Pop!* A moment more and he was all rounded out: head and body, arms and legs. But not his right foot. That foot stayed flat.

Arthur stopped pumping. 'It's like trying to do the very last bit of those long balloons,' he said. 'Maybe a shake would help.'

Stanley shook his right foot twice, and with a little *whooshing* sound it swelled out to match the left one. There stood Stanley Lambchop as he used to be, as if he had never been flat at all!

'Thank you, Arthur,' Stanley said. 'Thank you very much.'

The brothers were shaking hands when Mr Lambchop strode into the room with Mrs Lambchop right behind him. 'We heard you!' said Mr Lambchop. 'Up and talking when you ought to be asleep, eh? Shame on—'

'GEORGE!' said Mrs Lambchop. 'Stanley's *round* again!'

'You're right!' said Mr Lambchop, noticing. 'Good for you, Stanley!'

'I'm the one who did it,' Arthur said. 'I blew him up.'

Everyone was terribly excited and happy, of course. Mrs Lambchop made

hot chocolate to celebrate the occasion, and several toasts were drunk to Arthur for his cleverness.

When the little party was over, Mr and Mrs Lambchop tucked the boys back into their beds and kissed them, and then they turned out the light. 'Good night,' they said.

'Good night,' said Stanley and Arthur.

It had been a long and tiring day. Very soon all the Lambchops were asleep.

STANLEY
AND THE MAGIC LAMP

Illustrated by Quentin Blake

Contents

Prologue   67

The First Day
Chapter One   74
Chapter Two   83

The Second Day
Chapter Three   98
Chapter Four   116
Chapter Five   135

For Elizabeth Tobin

Prologue

Once upon a very long time ago, way before the beginning of today's sort of people, there was a magical kingdom in which everyone lived forever, and anyone of importance was a genie, mostly the friendly kind. The few wicked genies kept out of sight in mountain caves or at the bottoms of rivers. They had no wish to provoke the great Genie King, who ruled very comfortably from an enormous palace with many towers and courtyards, and gardens with reflecting pools.

The Genie King took a special interest in the genie princes of the kingdom, and was noted for his patience with their high spirits and desire for adventure. The Genie Queen, in fact, thought he was *too* patient with them, and she said so one morning in the throne room, where the King was studying reports

and proposals for new magic spells.

'Training, that's what they need. Discipline!' She adjusted the Magic Mirror on the throne-room wall. 'Florts and collibots! Granting wishes, which is what they'll be doing one day, is serious work.'

'Florts yourself! You're too hard on these lads,' said the Genie King, and then he frowned. 'This report here, though, says that one of them has been behaving very badly indeed.'

'Haraz, right?' said the Queen. 'He's the worst. What a smarty!'

The Genie King sent a thought to summon Prince Haraz, which is all such a ruler has to do when he wants somebody, and a moment later the young genie flew into the throne room, did a triple flip, and hovered in the air before the throne.

'That's no way to present yourself!' The Queen was furious. 'Really!'

Prince Haraz grinned. 'What's up?'

'You are!' said the King. 'Come down here!'

'No problem,' said the Prince, landing.

'It seems you have been playing a great many magical jokes,' said the King, tapping the reports before him. 'Very *annoying* jokes, such as causing the army's carpets to fly only in circles, which made all my soldiers dizzy.'

'That was a good one!' laughed the Prince.

'And turning the Chief Wizard's wand into a sausage while he was casting a major spell, you did that?'

'Ha, ha! You should have seen his face!' said the Prince.

'Stop laughing!' cried the Queen. 'Oh, this is shameful! You should be heavily punished!'

'He's just a boy, dear, only two hundred years old,' said the King. 'But I'll –'

'Who knows what *more* he's done?' said the Queen, turning to the Magic Mirror. 'Magic Mirror, what other silly jokes has this fellow played?'

The Magic Mirror squirted apple juice all over her face and the front of her dress.

'Oooooohh!' The Queen whirled around. 'Florts and collibots! I know who's responsible for *that*!'

Prince Haraz blushed and tried to look

sorry, but it was too late.

'That does it!' said the Genie King. 'Lamp duty for you, you rascal! One thousand years of service to a lamp.' He turned to the Queen. 'How's that, my dear?'

'Make it two thousand,' said the Queen, drying her face.

The First Day
Chapter One

Almost a year had passed since Stanley Lambchop got over being flat, which he had become when his big bulletin board settled on him during the night. It had been a pleasant, restful time for all the Lambchops, as this particular evening was.

Dinner was over. In the living room, Mr Lambchop was reading and Mrs Lambchop was mending socks.

'How nice this is, my dear,' Mr Lambchop said. 'I am enjoying my newspaper, and your company, and the thought of our boys studying in their room.'

'Let us hope they *are* studying, George,' said Mrs Lambchop. 'So often they find excuses not to work.'

Mr Lambchop chuckled. 'They are very

imaginative,' he said. 'No doubt of that.'

In their bedroom, Stanley and his younger brother, Arthur, had in fact begun their homework. They wore pyjamas, and over his Arthur also wore his Mighty Man T-shirt, which helped him to concentrate.

On the desk between them was what they supposed to be a teapot – a round, rather squashed-down pot with a curving spout, and a knob on top for lifting. A wave had rolled it up onto the beach that summer, right to Stanley's feet, and since Mrs Lambchop was very fond of old furniture and silverware, he had saved it as a gift for her birthday, now only a week away.

The pot was painted dark green, but streaks of brownish metal showed through where the green had rubbed off. To see if polishing would make it shine, Stanley rubbed the knob with his pyjama sleeve.

Puff! Black smoke came from the spout.

'Yipe!' Arthur said. 'It's going to explode!'

'Teapots don't explode.' Stanley rubbed again. 'I just –'

Puff! Puff! Puff! They came rapidly now,

joining to form a small cloud in the air above the desk.

'Look out!' Arthur shouted. 'Double yipes!'

The black cloud swirled within itself, and its blackness became a mixture of brown and blue. A moment more, and it began to lose its cloud shape; arms appeared, and legs, and a head.

'Ready or not, here I come!' said a clear young voice.

And then the cloud was completely gone, and a slender, cheerful-looking boy hovered

in the air above the desk. He wore a sort of decorated towel on his head, a loose blue shirt, and curious, flapping brown trousers, one leg of which had snagged on the pot's spout.

'Florts!' said the boy, shaking his leg. 'Collibots! I got the puffs right, and the scary cloud, but – There!' Unsnagged, he floated down to the floor and bowed to Stanley and Arthur.

'Who rubbed?' he asked.

Neither of the brothers could speak.

'Well, *someone* did. Genies don't just drop in, you know.' The boy bowed again. 'How do you do? I am Prince Fawzi Mustafa Aslan Mirza Melek Namerd Haraz. Call me Prince Haraz.'

Arthur gasped and dived under his bed.

'What's the matter with him?' the genie asked. 'And who are you, and where am I?'

'I'm Stanley Lambchop, and this is the United States of America,' Stanley said. 'That's my brother Arthur under the bed.'

'Not a very friendly welcome,' said Prince Haraz. 'Especially for someone who's been cooped up in a lamp.' Frowning, he rubbed the back of his neck. 'Florts! One thousand years, with my knees right up against my chin. This is my first time out.'

'I must have gone crazy,' said Arthur from

under the bed. 'I am just going to lie here until a doctor comes.'

'Actually, Prince Haraz, you're here sort of by accident,' Stanley said. 'I didn't even know that pot was a lamp. Was it the rubbing? Those puffs of smoke, I mean, that turned into you?'

'Were you scared?' The genie laughed. 'Just a few puffs, I thought, and then I'll *whoooosh* up the spout!'

'Scaring *me* wasn't fair,' said Arthur, staying under the bed. 'I just live in this room because Stanley's my brother. It's his lamp, and he's the one who rubbed it.'

'Then he's the one I grant wishes for,' said Prince Haraz. 'Too bad for you.'

'I don't care,' said Arthur, but he did.

'Can I wish for anything?' Stanley asked. 'Anything at all?'

'Not if it's cruel or evil, or really nasty,' said Prince Haraz. 'I'm a lamp genie, you see, and we're the good kind. Not like those big jar genies. They're stinkers! Take my advice and stay away from big jars and urns – and if you do see one, don't rub it.'

'Wish for something, Stanley,' said Arthur, sounding suspicious. 'Test him out.'

'Wait,' Stanley said. 'I'll be right back.'

He went out into the living room, where Mr and Mrs Lambchop were still sitting quietly, enjoying themselves.

'Hey!' he said. 'Guess what?'

'Hay is for horses, Stanley, not people,' said Mr Lambchop from behind his newspaper. 'Try to remember that.'

'Excuse me,' Stanley said. 'But you'll never guess –'

'My guess is that you and Arthur have not yet finished your homework,' said Mrs Lambchop, looking up from her mending. 'In fact, you can hardly have begun.'

'We *were* going to do it,' said Stanley, talking very fast, 'but I have this pot that turned out to be a lamp, and when I rubbed it smoke came out and then a genie, and he says I can wish for things, only I thought maybe I should ask you first. Arthur got scared, so he's hiding under the bed.'

Mr Lambchop chuckled. 'When your studying is done, my boy,' he said. 'But no treasure chests full of gold and diamonds, please. Think of the taxes we would pay!'

'There is your answer, Stanley,' said Mrs Lambchop. 'Now back to work, please.'

'Okay, then,' said Stanley, going out.

Mrs Lambchop laughed. 'Chests full of gold and diamonds, indeed. Taxes! George, you are very amusing.'

Behind his newspaper, Mr Lambchop smiled again. 'Thank you, my dear,' he said.

Chapter Two

'I told them, but they didn't believe me,' Stanley said, back in the bedroom.

'Of course they didn't.' Arthur was still under the bed. 'Who'd believe that a whole person could puff out of a pot?'

'It's not a *pot*,' said Prince Haraz. 'And this is a ridiculous way to carry on a conversation. Please come out. I apologize for the puffs.'

Arthur crawled from under the bed. 'No more scary stuff?'

'I promise,' the genie said, and they shook hands.

Arthur could hardly wait now. 'Try it, Stanley,' he said. 'Try a wish.'

'We're not allowed,' Stanley said. 'Not till our homework is done.'

'What's homework?' Prince Haraz asked.

The brothers stared at him, amazed, and then Stanley explained. The genie shook his head.

'*After* schooltime, when you could be having fun?' he said. 'Where I come from, we just let Askit Baskets do the work.'

'Well, whatever *they* are, I wish I had one,' said Stanley, forgetting he was not supposed to wish.

Prince Haraz laughed. 'Oh? Look behind you.'

Turning, Stanley and Arthur saw a large straw basket, about the size of a beach ball and decorated with green and red zigzag stripes, floating in the air above the desk.

'Yipes!' said Arthur. 'More scary stuff!'

'Don't be silly,' said the genie. 'It's a perfectly ordinary Askit Basket. Whatever you want to know, Stanley, just ask it.'

Feeling rather foolish, Stanley leaned forward and spoke to the basket.

'I, uh . . . that is . . . uh,' he said. 'I'd like, uh . . . can I have the answers for my maths homework? It's the problems on page twenty of my book.'

The basket made a steady *huuuummm* sound, and then the hum stopped and a man's voice rose from it, deep and rich like a TV announcer's.

'Thank you for calling Askit Basket,' it said. 'Unfortunately, all our Answer Genies are busy at the present time, but your questions have been received, and you will be served by the first available personnel. While you wait, enjoy a selection by The Genie-ettes. This message will not be repeated.'

Stanley stared at the Askit Basket. Music was coming out of it now, the sort of soft, faraway music he had heard in the elevators of big office buildings.

Prince Haraz shrugged. 'What can you do? It's a very popular service.'

There was a *click* and the music stopped. Now a female voice, full of bouncy good cheer, came from the basket. 'Hi! This is Shireen. Thanks a whole bunch for waiting, and I would like at this time to give you your answers. The first answer is: 5 pears, 6 apples, 8 bananas. The second answer is: Tom is 4 years old, Tim is 7, Ted is 11. The third –'

'Let me get a pencil!' Stanley shouted. 'I can't remember all this!'

'A written record, created especially for your own personal convenience, is in the basket, sir,' said the cheery voice. 'Thanks for calling Askit Basket, and have a nice day!'

'Wait!' Lifting the lid of the basket, Stanley saw a sheet of paper with all his answers on it. 'Oh, good!' he said. 'Thank you. Can my brother talk now, please?'

Arthur cleared his throat. 'Hello, Shireen,' he said. 'This is Arthur Lambchop speaking. For English, I'm supposed to write about "What I Want to Be." Could I have it printed out, please, like Stanley's maths?'

The answer came right away. 'Certainly, Mr Lambchop. Just a teeny-tiny moment

now, while we make sure the handwriting –
There! All done, Mr Lambchop!'

Arthur opened the basket and found a
sheet of lined paper covered with his own
handwriting. He read it aloud.

WHAT I WANT TO BE
by Arthur Lambchop.

When I grow up, I want to be President of
the United States so that I can make a
law not to have any more wars. And get to
meet astronauts. And I would like to be
handsome, only not have to go out with
girls who want to get all dressed up. Most
of all I would like to be the strongest man
in the world, like Mighty Man, not to
hurt people, but so everybody would be
extra nice to me.

The End.

Arthur smiled. 'That's pretty good!' he
said. 'Just what I wanted to say, Shireen.'

'I'm so glad,' said the Askit Basket. 'Bye-bye now!'

Stanley and Arthur called good-bye, and then Prince Haraz plucked the basket out of the air and set it on the desk beside his lamp.

'There! Homework's done,' he said. 'That was an awfully ordinary sort of wish, Stanley. Isn't there something special you've always wanted? Something exciting?'

Stanley knew right away what he wanted most. He had always loved animals; how exciting it would be to have his own zoo! But that would take up too much space, he thought. Just one animal then, a truly unusual pet. A lion? Yes! What fun it would be to walk down the street with a pet lion on a leash!

'I wish for a lion!' he said. 'Real, but friendly.'

'Real, but friendly,' said the genie. 'No problem.'

Stanley realized suddenly that a lion would scare people, and that an elephant would be even greater fun.

'An elephant, I mean!' he shouted. 'Not a

lion. An elephant!'

'What?' said Prince Haraz. 'An eleph–? Oh, collibots! Look what you made me do!'

A most unusual head had formed in the air across the room, a head with an elephant's trunk for a nose, but with small, neat, lion-like ears. A lion's mane appeared behind the head, but then came an elephant's body and legs in a brownish-gold lion colour, and finally a little grey elephant tail with a pretty gold ruff at the tip. All together, these parts made an animal about the size of a medium lion or a small elephant.

'My goodness!' said Stanley. 'What's that?'

'A Liophant.' Prince Haraz sounded annoyed. 'It's your fault, not mine. You overlapped your wish.'

The Liophant opened his mouth wide and went *Grrowll-HONK!* a half roar, half snort that made everyone jump. Then he sat back on his hind legs and went *pant-pant-pant* like a puppy, looking quite nice.

'Well, we got the friendly part right,' said the genie. 'The young ones mostly are.'

Stanley patted him, and Arthur tickled behind the neat little ears. The Liophant licked their hands, and Stanley was not at all sorry that he had mixed up his wish.

Just then, a knock sounded on the bedroom door, and Mrs Lambchop's voice called out, 'Homework done?'

'Come in,' Stanley said, not stopping to think, and the door opened.

'How very quiet you –' Mrs Lambchop began, and then she stopped.

Her eyes moved slowly about the room from Prince Haraz to the Askit Basket, and on to the Liophant.

'Gracious!' she said.

Prince Haraz made a little bow. 'How do you do? You are the mother of these fine lads, I suppose?'

'I am, thank you,' said Mrs Lambchop. 'Have we met? I don't seem to –'

'This is Prince Haraz,' Stanley said. 'And

that's a Liophant, and that's an Askit Basket.'

'Guess what,' said Arthur. 'Prince Haraz is a genie, and he'll let Stanley have anything he wants.'

'How very generous!' Mrs Lambchop said. 'But I'm not sure . . .' Turning, she called into the living room. 'George, you had better come here! Something quite unexpected has happened.'

'In a moment,' Mr Lambchop called back. 'I am reading an unusual story in my newspaper, about a duck who watches TV.'

'This is even more unusual than that,' she said, and Mr Lambchop came at once.

'Ah, yes,' he said, looking about the room. 'Yes, I see. Would someone care to explain?'

'I tried to before,' Stanley said. 'Remember? About the lamp, and –'

'Wait, dear,' said Mrs Lambchop.

The Liophant was making snuffling, hungry sounds, so she went off to the kitchen and returned with a large bowl full of hamburger mixed with warm milk. While the Liophant ate, Stanley told what had happened.

'Unusual indeed! And what a fine opportunity for you, Stanley,' Mr Lambchop said when he had heard everything, and then he frowned. 'But I do not approve of using the Askit Basket for homework, boys. Nor will your teachers, I'm afraid.'

'My plan is, let's not tell them,' Arthur said.

Mr Lambchop gave him a long look. 'Would you take credit for work you have not done?'

Arthur blushed. 'Oh, no! When you put it that way ... Gosh, of course not! I wasn't thinking. Because of all the excitement, you know?'

Mr Lambchop wrote NOT IN USE on a piece of cardboard and taped it to the Askit Basket.

'It is too late for any more wishing tonight,' said Mrs Lambchop. 'Prince Haraz, there is a folding bed in the cupboard, so you will be quite comfortable here with Stanley and Arthur. Tomorrow is Saturday, which we Lambchops always spend together in the park. You will join us, I hope?'

'Thank you very much,' said the genie, and he helped Stanley and Arthur set up the bed.

The Liophant was already asleep, and after Mr and Mrs Lambchop had said good night, Mrs Lambchop picked up his bowl. 'Gracious!' she said, putting out the light. 'Three

pounds of the best hamburger, and he ate it all!'

It was quite dark in the bedroom, but some moonlight shone through the window. From their beds, Stanley and Arthur could see that Prince Haraz was still sitting up on his. For a moment they all kept silent, listening to the gentle snoring of the Liophant, and then the genie said, 'Sorry about that. It's having all that nose, probably.'

'It's okay,' Arthur said sleepily. 'Do genies snore?'

'We don't even sleep,' said Prince Haraz. 'Your mother was so kind, I didn't want to tell her. It might have made her feel bad.'

'I'll try to stay awake for a while, if you want to talk,' Stanley said.

'No thanks,' the genie said. 'I'll be fine. After all those years alone in the lamp, it's nice just having company.'

The Second Day
Chapter Three

Everyone slept late and enjoyed a large breakfast, particularly the Liophant, who ate two
more pounds of hamburger, five bananas,
and three loaves of bread.

Then, since all the Lambchops enjoyed
playing tennis, they set out with their rackets
for the courts in the big park close by. Since
his genie clothes would make people stare,
Prince Haraz borrowed slacks and a shirt
from Stanley, and came along to watch.

In the street, they met Ralph Jones, an old
college friend of Mr Lambchop's, whom they
had not seen for quite some time.

'Nice running into you, George, and you
too, Mrs Lambchop,' Mr Jones said. 'Hello,
Arthur. Hello, Stanley. Aren't you the one
who was flat? Rounded out nicely, I see.'

'You always did have a fine memory, Ralph,' Mr Lambchop said. 'Let me introduce our house guest, Prince Haraz. He is a foreign student, here to study our ways.'

'How do you do,' said the genie. 'I am Fawzi Mustafa Aslan Mirza Melek Namerd Haraz.'

'How do you do,' Mr Jones said. 'Well, I must be on my way. Good-bye, Lambchops. Nice to have met you, Prince Fawzi Mustafa Aslan Mirza Melek Namerd Haraz.'

'He *does* have a wonderful memory,' Mrs Lambchop said, as Mr Jones walked away.

They set out for the park again.

'Wouldn't Mr Jones be surprised if he learned Prince Haraz was a genie?' Mrs Lambchop said. 'The whole world would be amazed. Gracious! We'd all be famous, I'm sure.'

'I was famous once, when I was flat,' Stanley said. 'I didn't like it after a while.'

'I remember,' said Mrs Lambchop. 'Nevertheless, I would enjoy discovering for myself what being famous feels like.'

Prince Haraz looked at Stanley, his eyebrows raised in a questioning way. Stanley gave a little nod, and the genie smiled and nodded back.

Just ahead, near the entrance to the park, was the Famous Museum of Art, one of the most important buildings in the city. A guided-tour bus, filled with visitors from all over the United States and from many foreign countries, had stopped in front of the museum, and the driver was lecturing his passengers through a megaphone.

'Over where those trees are, that's our magnificent City Park!' shouted the driver. 'Here, on the right, is the Famous Museum of Art, with the world's most expensive paintings, statues, and – Oh, what a surprise! We're in luck today, folks! That's Mrs George Lambchop, coming right toward us! Harriet Lambchop herself, in person! Right there, with the tennis racket!'

Cries of astonishment and pleasure rose from the tourists as they turned in their seats to stare where the driver was pointing.

'What's this?' said Mr Lambchop. 'Is that man talking about you, Harriet?'

'I think so,' said Mrs Lambchop. 'Oh, my goodness! They're coming!'

The tourists were rushing out of the bus, waving cameras and autograph pads. A Japanese family reached Mrs Lambchop first, all with cameras.

'Please, Lambchop lady,' said the husband,

bowing politely. 'Honour to take picture, yes?'

'Of course,' said Mrs Lambchop. 'I hope you are enjoying our country. But why *my* picture? I'm not –'

'No, no! Famous, famous! Famous Lambchop lady!' cried the Japanese family, taking pictures as fast as they could.

Mrs Lambchop understood suddenly that her wish had been granted. 'Thank you, Stanley and Prince Haraz!' she said. 'What fun!'

She posed graciously for all the tourists and signed dozens of autographs. This took almost half an hour, and at the entrance to the park she was recognized again, and had to do more posing and signing.

It was by now mid-morning, and all the park's tennis courts were occupied, but the Lambchops' disappointment vanished quickly when they saw a crowd gathered by one court, and learned that Tom McRude, the world's best tennis player, was about to lecture and demonstrate his strokes. Tom McRude had a terrible temper and very bad manners, but because of his wonderful tennis

103

a great many people had come to see him. The Lambchops and Prince Haraz managed to squeeze close to the court, next to the television news cameras that were covering the event.

'None of you can ever be a great tennis player like me,' Tom McRude was saying, out on the court. 'But at least you can have the thrill of getting to see me.'

A little old lady in the crowd gave a tiny sneeze, and he glared at her. 'What's the matter with you, granny?' he shouted.

The old lady burst into tears, and her friends led her away.

'What a mean fellow!' Prince Haraz whispered to Stanley.

'I can't stand old sneezing people!' said Tom McRude. 'Okay, now I'm going to show how I hit my great forehand! First, I –'

'Hold it, Tom!' called the television director. 'We've just spotted Harriet Lambchop in the crowd here. What a break! Maybe we can get her to say a few words to our audience!'

Even Tom McRude was impressed. '*The* Harriet Lambchop? Here? In person?'

'Swing those cameras this way, fellows!' The director ran to where the Lambchops were standing, and held a microphone out to Mrs Lambchop.

'Wonderful to see you!' he said. 'Everybody wants to know what you think. What about the foreign situation? What's your favourite colour? Go to discos? Do you sleep in pyjamas or a nightdress?'

'Isn't that rather personal?' said Mr Lambchop.

'George, please....' Mrs Lambchop smiled at the director. 'Thank you for your kind welcome,' she said into the microphone, 'and I would just like to say at this time that I hope all my fans are having a lovely day here in this delightful park.'

The crowd cheered and waved, and Mrs Lambchop waved back and blew a few kisses. Tom McRude was so jealous of the attention she was getting that he whacked a tennis ball angrily over the trees behind the court. Noticing, Mrs Lambchop spoke again into the microphone.

'And now,' she said, 'do let us hear what this champion athlete has to tell us about tennis.'

'Yeah!' growled Tom McRude at the TV man. 'Get those cameras back on me!'

When the cameras had swung back to him again, he said, 'Now I want a volunteer, so that I can demonstrate how terrible most players are compared to me.'

Mr Lambchop thought how exciting it would be to venture onto the same court with the champion. Signalling with his racket, he stepped forward.

'Okay.' Tom McRude handed over some balls. 'Let's see how you serve.'

Mr Lambchop prepared to serve.

'He's got his feet wrong!' Tom McRude

shouted to the crowd. 'And his grip is wrong! Everything is wrong!'

This made Mr Lambchop so nervous that he served two balls into the net instead of over it.

'Terrible, terrible! Watch how I do it,' said Tom McRude, running to the far side of the court. From there, he served five balls in a row to Mr Lambchop, so hard and fast that Mr Lambchop missed the first four entirely. The fifth one knocked the racket out of his hand.

'Ha, ha!' laughed Tom McRude. 'Now let's see you run!'

He began hitting whizzing forehands and backhands at sharp angles across the court, making Mr Lambchop look very foolish indeed as he raced back and forth, getting redder and redder in the face and missing practically every shot.

The other Lambchops grew very angry as they watched, and Prince Haraz saw how they felt. 'This need not continue, you know,' he whispered to Stanley.

Just then, Mr Lambchop came skidding to

a halt before them, banging his knee with his racket as he missed another of the champion's powerful shots.

'Ha, ha! This is how *I* give lessons!' shouted Tom McRude.

Mr Lambchop's eyes met Stanley's, and then he looked at Prince Haraz.

'Okay,' Stanley said, and Prince Haraz smiled his little smile again.

'Thank you,' said Mr Lambchop. Returning to the court, he addressed the crowd. 'Ladies and gentlemen!' he said. 'I will try my serve again!'

Across the net, Tom McRude laughed a nasty laugh and slashed his big racket through the air.

Mr Lambchop served a ball, not into the net this time, but right where it was supposed to go, as fast as a bullet. Tom McRude could only blink as it went past him. Then his mouth fell open. 'Out!' he shouted. 'That ball was out!'

Voices rose from the crowd. 'Shame on you! . . . It was *in*! . . . What a liar! . . . In, in in!'

Tom McRude shook his fist at Mr Lambchop. 'I'll bet you can't do that again!'

Mr Lambchop served three more times, each serve even faster than the first one, and as perfectly placed. Tom McRude could not even touch them, except for the last, which bounced up into his nose.

Then Mr Lambchop began to rally with him, gliding swiftly about the court and returning every shot with ease. With powerful forehands and backhands, he made Tom McRude run from corner to corner; with little drop shots, he drew the champion up to the net, then lobbed marvellous high shots that sent him racing back again. Nobody has ever played such great tennis as Mr Lambchop played that day.

Tom McRude was soon too exhausted, and too angry, to continue. He threw down his racket and jumped on it, and hurled the broken pieces into the net.

'You're just lucky!' he yelled. 'Besides, I have a cold. And the sun was in my eyes the whole time!' He pushed his way through the crowd and ran out of the park.

There was tremendous clapping and cheering for Mr Lambchop, who just smiled modestly and waved his racket in a friendly way. Then he came over to where Stanley and Arthur and Mrs Lambchop and Prince Haraz were standing with the television director.

'You're really *good*,' the director said. 'Frankly, you looked terrible when you first went out there.'

'It takes me a while to get warmed up,' Mr Lambchop said, and led his family away.

In the excitement of the tennis, they had all forgotten Mrs Lambchop's fame, but on the way home she was asked again and again for her autograph, and when they arrived, a photographer and reporter from *Famous Faces* magazine were waiting.

'We want you on the cover of our next issue,' said the photographer.

'I'm supposed to do an interview,' said the reporter. 'Who do you think is sexy? How much do you weigh? Eat health foods? Will there be a movie about your life? Who gave you your first kiss?'

'None of your business!' said Mr Lambchop, and Mrs Lambchop told the *Famous Faces* people to go away.

They all watched the evening news on television, hoping Mr Lambchop's amazing tennis would be shown, but only Mrs Lambchop appeared, with Tom McRude in the background. 'The celebrated Harriet Lambchop was in the park today,' said the newscaster, after which there was a close-up of Mrs Lambchop saying, 'I hope all my fans are having a lovely day,' and that was that.

Mr Lambchop said he didn't care, but he did mind that dinner was interrupted several times by phone calls for Mrs Lambchop from newspaper and magazine and television people. The interruptions didn't bother the Liophant, who ate four pork chops, a jar of peanut butter, a quart of potato salad, and the rubber mat from under his dish.

Chapter Four

'I'm not complaining,' said Arthur, complaining, 'but it's not fair. Some people get to
have Liophants and be famous. I want to be
President, or as strong as Mighty Man, but
all I got was one minute with an Askit Basket
I'm not even allowed to use any more.'

He was talking to Stanley and Prince
Haraz. It was after dinner, and they were in
their bedroom, all in slippers and pyjamas.

'It's not my fault.' Prince Haraz looked
hurt. 'A genie just follows orders. Rub, I
appear. Wish, I grant. That's it.'

Stanley felt a little sorry for his brother. 'I
don't think you ought to be President,
Arthur,' he said. 'But I'll wish for you to be
the strongest man in the world.' He nodded to
Prince Haraz. 'Right now.'

'Oh, good!' Arthur said.

He waited, but nothing happened.

'Darn!' he said, 'I knew it wouldn't work!' Disappointed, he punched his left hand with his right fist.

'Owwwww!' Jumping up and down, he waved his hand to relieve the pain.

'When you're the strongest man in the world,' Prince Haraz said, 'you have to be careful what you hit.'

'But I still feel like me,' Arthur said. Testing himself, he took hold of the big desk with one hand and lifted. It rose easily into the air above his head.

Stanley's mouth flew open, and so did the desk drawers. Pencils, paper clips, marbles, and other odds and ends rained down onto the floor.

'Oooops,' Arthur said, and lowered the desk.

'This is ridiculous,' said Prince Haraz, helping him to tidy up. 'The strongest man in the world, in his bedroom picking up desks! Out having adventures, that's where you ought to be.'

'We can't have adventures now,' Arthur said. 'It's almost bedtime.'

Stanley had an idea. 'There'd be time if we could fly! Why can't we all fly somewhere?'

'I've always been able,' said Prince Haraz. 'For you two, it'll take wishing.'

'I wish!' Stanley shouted. 'Flying! Arthur and me both!'

Full of excitement, the brothers held their breath, thinking they would be swept up into the air, but they weren't. After a moment, Arthur tried a few small flapping movements with his elbows.

'Oh, collibots!' said the genie. 'Not like that. Just *think* of flying, and where you want to go.'

It worked.

Stanley and Arthur found themselves suddenly a few feet off the floor, facedown and quite comfortable, and however they wished to go, up or down, forward or back, was the way they went. It was like swimming in soft, invisible water, but without the effort of swimming. After only a few minutes of practice, the brothers were gliding happily about

the bedroom, with Prince Haraz giving advice: 'Point your toes, that helps. . . . Heads up. . . . Good, very good. Yes, I think you're ready now.'

He opened the window and leaned out. 'Nice enough,' he said. 'But there may be coolish winds higher up. We'd better wear something extra.'

Stanley and Arthur put on dressing-gowns and gloves, and the genie borrowed a red parka and a woollen dragon-face ski mask.

'Away we go!' he said, and the brothers floated through the window after him, out into the night.

Up! Up! Up! UP! they went, levelling off now and then to practise speeding, but mostly rising steadily higher. Stanley and Arthur flew side by side, gaining confidence from each other, and the genie kept an eye on them from behind.

It was a beautiful night. The sky above them was full of stars, and the lights of the city, far below, twinkled as brightly as the stars. The brothers' white dressing-gowns shone in the moonlight, and the genie's parka was a glowing red.

They flew above the big park, where an orchestra was giving a concert. Music floated up to them: the clear, sweet tones of flutes and violins and trumpets; the deep, strong notes of cymbals and drums.

'Oh, I'm enjoying this!' Prince Haraz called through his dragon mask. 'So different from inside that lamp!'

They joined hands and circled together, swooping and swaying in time to the music, going round and round above the blaze of light from where the orchestra sat. It was like ice-skating to music at a rink, but much more fun.

In the distance, the blinking wing lights of a big aeroplane moved steadily across the sky.

'Let's chase it!' Stanley shouted.

'Go on! I'll catch up!' Prince Haraz laughed and let them go.

Whoooosh! Whoooosh! With their arms by their sides, Stanley and Arthur flashed like rockets across the sky. Their dressing-gowns made little flapping sounds, like the sails of a boat racing before the wind.

The big aeroplane was fast, but the brothers were much faster. When they caught up, they were able to fly all around the plane, looking through the windows at the passengers reading and eating from tiny trays.

Arthur saw a little girl reading a comic magazine. Zooming in close to her window, he stretched his neck, trying to read over her shoulder. The little girl looked up and saw him. Being mean, she held the magazine down between her knees where he couldn't

see it, and then she stuck out her tongue.
Arthur stuck his tongue out at her, and the
little girl scowled and pulled the curtain
across her window.

On the other side of the plane, Stanley saw
a young couple with a crying baby across
their laps. They looked very tired, but they

were being kept awake. Stanley flew up next to the window so that the baby could see him over its parents' shoulders, and then he made a funny face, puffing out his lips and wrinkling his nose. The baby smiled, and Stanley put his thumbs in his ears and wriggled his other fingers. The baby smiled again, and closed its eyes and went to sleep.

Stanley flew around the plane, past the cockpit, to join Arthur on the other side.

There were two pilots in the cockpit, and one of them saw Stanley fly by. Turning his head slowly, he saw both brothers hovering above a wing tip, waiting for Prince Haraz to catch up.

'Guess what I see out there, Bert,' he said.

'The stars in the sky, Max, and below us the mighty ocean,' answered the other pilot.

'No,' said Max. 'Two kids in dressing-gowns.'

'Ha, ha! You are some joker!' said Bert, but he turned to look.

Only Prince Haraz could be seen now above the wing, his parka flapping as he looked around for Stanley and Arthur, who were hiding from him behind the plane.

'So what do you see, Bert?' asked Max, keeping his own eyes straight ahead. 'Two kids in dressing-gowns, right?'

'Wrong,' said Bert quietly. 'I see a guy in ski clothes with a dragon face.'

The two pilots stared at each other, and then looked out at the wing again, but the genie had flown to join the boys behind the plane.

'Nobody there,' said Max. 'Let's never mention this to anyone, Bert. Okay?'

'Good idea,' Bert answered. 'Definitely.'

They made the plane go faster and had nothing more to say.

A giant ocean liner, ablaze with lights, made its way across the sea below.

'Come on!' Arthur shouted. He whizzed away, Stanley behind him, and again Prince Haraz laughed and let them go.

The size and beauty of the great ship made the brothers cry out in wonder as they drew near. It was like an enormous birthday cake, each deck a layer sparkling with the brightness of a thousand candles.

'Look, Stanley!' Arthur pointed. 'They're having a big party on the main deck!'

They flew closer to enjoy the fun, and then they saw that it was not a party, but a robbery.

The main deck was crowded because masked robbers had lined up all 'the passengers, and were taking their money and jewellery and watches. The helicopter in which the robbers had landed was parked just below the captain's bridge, which overlooked the main deck. The captain and the other ship's officers had been chained up on the bridge. They had struggled, but now there was nothing they could do.

'We've got to help, Stanley!' Arthur said.

He zoomed down to the bridge, and shouted over the railing at the robbers on the deck below. 'Stop, you crooks! Give back all that money and jewellery and other stuff!'

Using his great strength, Arthur tore away the ropes and chains that bound the ship's officers. It was as easy for him as if he were tearing up paper.

The robbers were amazed. Unable to believe their eyes, they stumbled back from their victims, dropping money and jewellery all over the deck.

'Oh, lordy!' one robber yelled. 'Who are you?'

Remembering his favourite comic-magazine hero, Arthur could not resist showing off. He flew ten feet up in the air and stayed there, looking fierce.

'I am Mighty Arthur!' he shouted in a deep

voice. 'Mighty Arthur, Enemy of Crime!'

Exclamations rose from the robbers and passengers and ship's officers. 'So strong, and a flier too! . . . Who expected Mighty Arthur? . . . Are we ever lucky! . . . This ought to be on TV!'

Now Stanley came swooping down from the sky with his dressing-gown belt untied, so that the gown flared behind him like a cape.

'And I'm Mighty Stanley!' he called. "Defender of the Innocent!'

'I do that too!' cried Arthur, wishing he had made his robe a cape. 'We both do good things, but I'm the really strong one!'

Several robbers were trying to escape in the helicopter, and he saw another chance to prove his strength.

The helicopter was already rising, but Arthur flashed through the air until he was directly above it, and with one hand he pushed it back onto the deck. When the frightened robbers jumped out, the ship's officers grabbed them and tied them up.

Now the passengers were even more excited and amazed. 'Did you see that?' they

said, and 'Mighty Arthur and Mighty Stanley, both on the same day!' and 'This is *better* than TV!'

The brothers flew up to join Prince Haraz, who had been circling over the ship. 'What a pair of show-offs!' said the genie, as they set out for home. 'Even worse than I used to be.'

Behind them, cheers floated up from the grateful passengers and crew. 'Hooray for our rescuers!' they heard, and 'Especially Mighty Arthur!' which was followed a moment later by 'Mighty Stanley too, of course!'

Soon the big ship was no more than an outline of tiny lights in the black sea below, and the last cheer was only a whisper above the rushing of the wind. 'Three cheers … for … the Enemy … of … Crime … and the … Defender … of the Inno … cent!'

The brothers felt very proud, but it had been a tiring adventure, and they were not sorry when the city came into sight.

Chapter Five

When the three adventurers flew back into the bedroom, the Liophant was just finishing an enormous bowl of spaghetti mixed with chocolate cookies and milk. He looked sleepy, but Mr and Mrs Lambchop, standing by the door, were very much awake.

'Thank goodness you are all right!' Mrs Lambchop ran to hug her sons.

Mr Lambchop's voice was stern. 'Where have you been? Is that you, Prince Haraz, behind that dragon face?'

The genie took off his ski mask. 'Were you worried?' he said. 'Sorry. We just went for a little flight.'

'Wait till you hear!' said Arthur. 'You can't tell from looking, but I'm the strongest man in the world, and –'

'First take off those dressing-gowns and gloves,' said Mrs Lambchop. 'It is not wise to get overheated.'

She went on talking while they put their things away. 'What a *dreadful* evening! The phone never stopped ringing. I was asked to go on six television shows, and to be in an advertisement for a new kind of soap – they wanted pictures of me in the bathtub, so of course I said no! – and to sit with the mayor during the next parade. I'm exhausted! And such a fright, after all that, to find the window open and the three of you gone!'

'We thought we'd be right back,' said Stanley, apologizing. 'We didn't know so many exciting things would happen.'

Everyone sat down, and he explained about wishing Arthur strong, and the flying, not leaving out how they had chased the aeroplane and startled the robbers on the great ship at sea. Mr and Mrs Lambchop looked more and more worried as they listened, and when Stanley was done, Mr Lambchop gave a deep sigh.

'It seems, Prince Haraz,' he said, 'that there are often unexpected consequences when wishes come true.'

The genie nodded. 'I'll say. That's how I got myself put into a lamp.'

'It is not just the difficulty about the Askit Basket,' Mr Lambchop said. 'Mrs Lambchop has been famous for only a day, and already it has exhausted her and cost our family its privacy. And though Tom McRude deserved the lesson he got, his tennis comes from natural ability, and I am not proud of having shamed him by the use of magic.'

'And now Arthur is so strong that other boys will be afraid to play with him,' said Mrs Lambchop. 'And this flying, and getting mixed up with criminals – Oh, it *is* worrying!'

'Indeed it is,' Mr Lambchop said. 'We must all think hard about what has happened, and what the future may bring.'

'I will make hot chocolate,' said Mrs Lambchop. 'It is extremely helpful when there is serious thinking to be done.'

Everyone enjoyed the delicious hot chocolate she brought from the kitchen, with a marshmallow for each cup. Mr and Mrs Lambchop and Stanley and Arthur sat with their eyes half closed, sipping and thinking. Prince Haraz kept silent for a while, and then he said he was sorry to have caused problems, and began to pace up and down. The Liophant went to sleep.

At last Mr Lambchop put down his cup and cleared his throat. 'May I have your attention, please?' he said.

When they were all looking at him, he said, 'Here is my opinion. Genies and their magic,

Prince Haraz, may be well suited to faraway lands and long-ago times, but the Lambchops have always been quite ordinary people, and this is the United States of America, and the time is today. We are all grateful, I'm sure, for the excitement you have brought us, but I now believe that it would have been better for everyone if you had remained in your lamp. And so I must ask: Is it possible for Stanley to unwish the wishes he has made?'

'There is a way, actually,' said Prince Haraz, looking surprised.

Mrs Lambchop clapped her hands. 'How very wise you are, George! Don't you agree, boys?'

Arthur wasn't sure. 'I really like the flying,' he said, and then he sighed. 'But being so strong ... I guess nobody *would* play with me.'

'What I care most about is the Liophant,' Stanley said. 'Couldn't we just keep him?'

'He *is* very lovable,' Mrs Lambchop said. 'But he *eats* so much! We cannot afford to keep him.'

'Sad, my dear, but true,' said Mr Lambchop. 'Now tell us, Prince Haraz, how we are to proceed.'

'It's called Reverse Wishing,' said the genie.

The little green lamp was still on the desk, and he picked it up and turned it over. 'The instructions should be right here,' he said. 'Let's see....'

The Lambchops waited anxiously as he studied the words that had been carved into the bottom of the lamp.

'Simple enough,' he said, after a moment. 'Each wish has to be reversed separately. I just say "Mandrono!" and –' His voice rose. 'Oh, collibots! Double florts! See that little circle there? This is a training lamp! There may not be enough wishes left!'

'What?' exclaimed Mr Lambchop. 'What's a training lamp?'

'They're used for beginners like me, so we don't do too much for one person,' Prince Haraz said unhappily. 'The number in the circle, the fifteen, that's all the wishes I'm allowed to grant Stanley.'

The Lambchops all spoke at once. 'What? ... Only fifteen? ... You never said! ... Oh dear!'

'Please, I'm embarrassed enough,' said the genie, very red in the face. 'A training lamp! As if I were a baby!'

'We are all beginners at one time or another,' Mr Lambchop said. 'What matters now is, are fifteen wishes enough?'

Prince Haraz counted, folding his fingers to be sure he got it right. 'Askit Basket, Liophant – lucky he doesn't count double –

that's two, and fame for Mrs Lambchop and the fancy tennis, that's four. Making Arthur strong, five, and flying for him *and* Stanley is two more ...' He smiled. 'Seven, and seven for the reversing is fourteen! And we have a wish left over for some sort of good-bye treat!'

'Thank goodness!' said Mrs Lambchop.

'Could you manage all the reversing right now, please? It has grown very late.'

'I'll do the whole family in a bunch,' said the genie. 'Let's see.... Strength, famous, tennis, two flying. Ready, Arthur? No more Mighty Man after this, I'm afraid.'

'Will I feel weak?' Arthur asked. 'Will I flop over?'

The genie shook his head. 'Mandrono!' he said. 'Mandrono, Mandrono, Mandrono, Mandrono!'

Arthur felt a curious but not unpleasant prickling on the back of his neck. When the prickling stopped, he gave the big desk a shove, but it didn't move.

'I'm just the regular me again,' he said. 'Oh, well.'

'And I am just Harriet Lambchop again,' said Mrs Lambchop, smiling. 'An unimportant person.'

'To all of us, my dear, you are the most important person we know,' Mr Lambchop said. 'Arthur, you are as strong as you were yesterday. Think of it that way.'

Prince Haraz sipped the last of his hot

chocolate. 'Where was I? Oh, yes ...' He glanced at the Askit Basket, said, 'Mandrono!' and the basket was gone. 'That leaves just the Liophant,' he said.

The Lambchops all turned to look at the Liophant, who was awake now and sitting up in the corner, trying to scratch behind his lion ears with the tip of his elephant trunk. Stanley went over and patted him, and the Liophant licked his hand.

'How sweet!' said Mrs Lambchop. 'George, perhaps....?'

'What makes Liophants happiest,' the genie said, 'is open spaces, and chasing unicorns, and wrestling with other Liophants.'

'Then send him where it's like that,' said Stanley, patting again. The Liophant vanished halfway through the pat.

For a moment no one spoke. Then Mr Lambchop put his hand on Stanley's shoulder in a sympathetic way. 'Good for you,' he said.

Stanley sat down to think about the one wish he had left, and Mrs Lambchop began to collect the hot-chocolate cups. 'Where will you go, Prince Haraz, when you leave us?' she asked.

'Right back into that stuffy little lamp,' said the genie. 'And then it's just wait, wait, wait! Another thousand years, at least. It's a punishment I got for playing too many tricks.

My friends warned me, but I wouldn't listen.'

Sighing, he handed Mrs Lambchop his empty cup. 'Mosef, Ali, Ben Sifa, little Fawz. Such wonderful fellows! I think of them when I'm alone in the lamp, the fun they must be having, the games, the freedom. . . .'

The genie's voice trembled, and he turned his head away. All the Lambchops felt very sorry for him.

Then Arthur had an idea. He ran across the room to whisper it to Stanley.

'Whispering?' said Mrs Lambchop. 'Where are your manners, dear?'

'Who cares?' Prince Haraz said crossly. 'Let's have that last wish, and I'll smoke back into my lamp.'

The brothers were smiling at each other.

'Good idea, right?' said Arthur.

'Oh, yes!' Stanley said.

He turned to the genie. 'Here is my last wish, Prince Haraz. I wish for you not to stay in the lamp, but to go back where you came from, so that you can be with your genie friends and have good times with them, forever from now on!'

Prince Haraz gasped. His mouth fell open.

Mr Lambchop worried that he might faint. 'Are you all right?' he asked. 'Is Stanley not allowed to set you free?'

'Oh, yes....' The genie's voice was very low. 'It's allowed. But whoever heard of ... That is, nobody ever used up a wish for the sake of a genie. Not until now.'

'How very selfish people can be!' said Mrs Lambchop.

Prince Haraz rubbed his eyes. 'What a fine family this is!' he said, beginning to smile. 'I thank you all. The name of Lambchop will be honoured always, wherever genies meet.'

His smile enormous now, he shook hands with each of the Lambchops. The last shake was with Stanley, and the genie was already a bit smoky about the edges. By the time he let go of Stanley's hand, he was all smoke, a dark cloud that swirled briefly over the little lamp on the desk, and then poured in through the spout until not a puff remained.

Full of wonder, the Lambchops gathered about the lamp, and after a moment Arthur put his lips to the spout.

'Good-bye, Prince Haraz!' he called. 'Have a nice trip!'

From inside the lamp, faint and far away, a voice cried, 'Bless you, bless you all ...' and then there was only silence in the room.

'I am proud of you, Stanley,' Mr Lambchop said. 'Your last wish was generous and kind.'

'It was my idea, actually,' Arthur said, and Mrs Lambchop kissed the top of his head.

Then she gathered the last of the hot-chocolate cups and put them on her tray. 'Off to bed now,' she said. 'Tomorrow is another day.'

Stanley and Arthur got into bed, and she turned out the light.

'The lamp was supposed to be a surprise birthday present,' Stanley said sleepily. 'Now it won't be a surprise anymore.'

'I will love my present when you give it to me,' said Mrs Lambchop. 'And Prince Haraz was a tremendous surprise. Good night, boys.'

She kissed them both, and so did Mr Lambchop, and they went out.

The brothers lay quietly in the darkness for a while, and then Stanley sighed. 'I miss the Liophant a little,' he said. 'But I don't mind about the rest.'

'Me neither,' Arthur yawned. 'Florts, Stanley, and good night.'

'Good night,' Stanley said. 'Collibots.'

'Mandrono,' murmured Arthur, and soon they were both asleep.

THE END

STANLEY IN SPACE

Illustrated by Philippe Dupasquier

Contents

The Call	157
Washington	163
Taking Off	170
In Space	173
The Tyrrans	184
Tyrra Ville	192
President Ot's Story	198
Stanley's Good Idea	204
The Weighing	208
Heading Home	214
Earth Again	218

For Dorothy Olding

'Will you meet with us?
Does anyone hear?'
From the great farness of space,
from farther than any planet or
star that has ever been mentioned
in books, the questions came.
Again and again.
'Will you meet with us?
Does anyone hear?'

CHAPTER ONE

The Call

It was Saturday morning, and Mr and Mrs Lambchop were putting up wallpaper in the kitchen.

'Isn't this nice, George?' said Mrs Lambchop, stirring paste. 'No excitement. A perfectly *usual* day.'

Mr Lambchop knew just what she meant. Excitement was often troublesome. The flatness of their son Stanley, for example, after his big bulletin board settled on him overnight. Exciting, but worrying too, till Stanley got round again. And that genie visiting, granting wishes. Oh, very exciting! But all the wishes had to be *unwished* before the genie returned to

157

the lamp from which he sprung.

'Yes, dear.' Mr Lambchop smoothed down wallpaper. 'Ordinary. The very best sort of day.'

In the living-room, Stanley Lambchop and his younger brother Arthur were watching a Tom Toad cartoon on TV. The sporty Toad was water-skiing and fell off, making a great splash. Arthur laughed so hard he didn't hear the telephone, but Stanley answered it.

'Lambchop residence?' said the caller. 'The President of the United States speaking. Who's this?'

Stanley smiled. 'The King of France.'

'They don't have kings in France. Not any more.'

'Excuse me, but I'm too busy for jokes.' Stanley kept his eyes on the TV. 'My brother and I are watching the Tom Toad Show.'

'Well, you *keep* watching, young fellow!' The caller hung up, just as Mr and Mrs Lambchop came in to watch the rest of the show.

'Hey, guess what?' Stanley said.

'Hay is for horses,' said Mrs Lambchop, mindful always of careful speech. 'Who called, dear?'

Stanley laughed. 'The President of the United States!'

Arthur laughed too. 'Stanley said *he* was the King of France!'

Tom Toad vanished suddenly from the TV screen, and an American flag appeared. 'We bring you a special message from the White House in Washington, D.C.,' said the deep voice of an announcer. 'Ladies and gentlemen, the President of the United States!'

The screen showed the President, looking very serious, behind his desk.

'My fellow Americans,' the President said. 'I am sorry to interrupt this programme, but someone out there doesn't realize that I am a

very busy man who can't waste time joking on the telephone. I hope the particular person I am talking to – and I do *not* mean the King of France! – will remember that. Thank you. Now here's The Toad Show again.'

Tom Toad, still water-skiing, came back on the TV.

'Stanley!' exclaimed Mrs Lambchop. 'The King of France indeed!'

'Gosh!' Arthur said. 'Will Stanley get put in jail?'

'There is no law against being a telephone smarty,' Mr Lambchop said. 'Perhaps there should be.'

The telephone rang, and he answered it. 'George Lambchop here.'

'Good!' It was the President. 'I've been trying to get hold of you!'

'Oh, my!' Mr Lambchop said. 'Please excuse –'

'Hold on. You're the fellow has the boy was flat once, got his picture in the newspaper?'

'My son Stanley, Mr President,' Mr Lambchop said, to let the others know who was calling.

'I had to be sure,' said the President. 'We have to get together, Lambchop! I'll send my private plane right now, fetch you all here to Washington, D.C.'

Mr Lambchop gasped. 'Private plane? Washington? *All* of us?'

'The whole family.' The President chuckled. 'Including the King of France.'

CHAPTER TWO

Washington

At the White House, in his famous Oval Office, the President shook hands with all the Lambchops.

'Thanks for coming.' He chuckled. 'Bet you never thought when you woke up this morning that you'd get to meet me.'

'Indeed not,' Mr Lambchop said. 'This is quite a surprise.'

'Well, here's another one,' said the President. 'The reason I asked you to come.'

He sat down behind his desk, serious now. 'Tyrra! Never heard of it, right?'

The Lambchops all shook their heads.

'*Nobody* ever heard of it. It's a planet, up

there somewhere. They sent a message, the first ever from outer space!'

The Lambchops were greatly interested. 'Imagine!' Mrs Lambchop exclaimed. 'What did it say?'

'Very friendly tone,' the President said. 'Peaceful, just checking around. Asked us to visit. Now, my plan –'

A side door of the Oval Office had opened suddenly to reveal a nicely dressed lady wearing a crown. Mrs Lambchop recognized her at once as the Queen of England.

'About the banquet, also the –' the Queen began, and saw that the President was busy.

'Ooops! We beg your pardon.' She closed the door.

'This place is a *madhouse*,' the President said. 'Visitors, fancy dinners, no end to it. Now, where –? Ah, yes! The *Star Scout*!'

He leaned forward.

'That's our new top-secret spaceship, just ready now! Send somebody up in the *Star Scout*, I thought, to meet with these Tyrrans. But who? Wouldn't look peaceful to send soldiers, or even scientists. Then I thought: What could be more peaceful than just an ordinary American boy?'

The President smiled. 'Why not Stanley

165

Lambchop?'

'Stanley?' Mrs Lambchop gasped. 'In a spaceship? To meet with an alien race?'

'Oh, boy!' said Stanley. 'I would love to go!'

'Me, too,' said Arthur. 'It's not fair if –'

'Arthur!' Mr Lambchop drew in a deep breath. 'Mr President, why *Stanley*?'

'It has to be someone that's already had adventure experience,' the President said. 'Well, my Secret Service showed me a newspaper story about when Stanley was flat and caught two robbers. Robbers! That's adventure!'

'I've had them too!' Arthur said. 'A genie taught me to fly, and we had a Liophant, and –'

'A *what*?'

'A Liophant,' Arthur said. 'Half lion, half elephant. They're nice.'

'Is that right? The Secret Service never –'

'Mr President?' Mrs Lambchop did not like to interrupt, but her concern was great.

'Mr President?' she said. 'This *mission*: Is it safe?'

'My goodness, of course it's safe!' the President said. 'We have taken great care, Mrs Lambchop. The *Star Scout* has all the latest scientific equipment. And it has been very carefully tested. First, we tried it on automatic pilot, with no passengers. It worked perfectly!

Even then, ma'am, we were not satisfied. We sent the *Star Scout* up again, this time with our cleverest trained bird aboard. But hear for yourself.' The President spoke into a little box on his desk. 'Send in Dr Schwartz, please.'

A bearded man entered, wearing a white coat and carrying a birdcage with a cloth over it. Bowing, he removed the cloth to reveal a large, brightly-coloured parrot.

'Thank you, Herman,' the President said. 'Dr Schwartz is our top space scientist,' he told the Lambchops, 'and this is Polly, the bird I spoke of. Polly, tell the folks here about your adventure into space.'

'Piece of cake,' said the parrot. 'Terrific! Loved every minute of it!'

'Thank you, Herman,' the President said, and Dr Schwartz carried Polly away.

'That was very reassuring, but it is out of the question for Stanley to go alone,' Mrs Lambchop said. 'However, we *were* planning a family vacation. Would it be possible, Mr President, for us all to go?'

'Well, if you didn't mind the crowding,' the President said. 'And skimped on baggage.'

'Actually, we had in mind the seaside,' Mr Lambchop said. 'Or a tennis camp. But –'

The Queen of England looked in again. 'May we ask if –'

'Just a *minute*, for heaven's sake!' said the President.

'We shall return anon.' Looking peeved, the Queen went away.

Mr Lambchop had decided. 'Mr President, the seaside will keep. We will go to Tyrra, sir.'

'Wonderful!' The President jumped up. 'To the stars, Lambchops! Some training at the Space Centre, and you're on your way!'

CHAPTER THREE

Taking Off

'Ten!' said the voice of Mission Control.

The count-down had begun. When it reached 'Zero' Chief Pilot Stanley Lambchop would press the 'Start' button, and the *Star Scout* would blast off for Tyrra.

'Nine!'

Strapped into their seats, the Lambchops held their breaths, each thinking very different thoughts.

Stanley was wondering if the Tyrrans would mind that Earth had sent just an ordinary family. Suppose they were big stuck-ups and expected a general or a TV star, or even the President? Suppose – 'Eight!' said Control, and Stanley fixed his eyes on the panel before him.

Mr Lambchop was thinking that serving one's country was noble, but this was a bit much. How did these things happen? Off to an unknown planet, the entire family! Other families didn't have a son become flat. Other families didn't find genies in the house. Other – Oh, well! Mr Lambchop sighed.

'Seven!' said Control.

Mrs Lambchop thought that Mr Lambchop seemed fretful. But why, now that the *Star Scout* looked so *nice*? Thanks to her, in fact. 'They may call it a spaceship,' she had said when she first saw it, 'but where's the *space*? Just one room! And all grey . . . ? Drab, I say!' Much of the training at the Space Centre, however, was physical, and Mrs Lambchop, who jogged and exercised regularly, quickly passed the tests required. In the days that followed, while the others were being made fit, she used her free time to make the *Star Scout* more like home. Only so much weight was permitted, but she managed a bathroom scale for the shower alcove and a plastic curtain, pretty shades for the portholes, a Venetian blind for the Magnifying Exploration Window, and posters of Mexico and France.

'Six! . . . Five! . . . Four! . . . Three! . . .'

Mrs Lambchop made sure her purse was snug beneath her seat.

Arthur, by nature lazy, was thinking that he was glad to be done with all the jogging, jumping, climbing ladders, and scaling walls. When he was super-strong, thanks to the genie, it would have been easy. But for just plain Arthur Lambchop, he thought, it was tiring.

'Two!' said Control. 'Good luck, everybody! One!'

'Pay attention, dear,' Mrs Lambchop told Stanley.

'Zero!' said Control, and Stanley pressed the 'Start' button.

Whrooom! Rockets roaring, the *Star Scout* rose from its launching pad.

Whroooooom! *Whroooooom*! Gaining speed, it soared higher and higher, carrying the Lambchops towards the farness where Tyrra lay.

CHAPTER FOUR

In Space

'I'll just flip this omelette,' said Mrs Lambchop, making breakfast in the *Star Scout*, 'and then – Oh, dear!' The omelette hovered like a Frisbee in the air above her.

Mostly, however, after weeks in space, the Lambchops remembered that gravity, the force that held things down, did not exist beyond Earth's atmosphere. Mr Lambchop often read now with his hands clasped behind his head, allowing his book to float before him, and Stanley and Arthur greatly enjoyed pushing from their chairs to drift like feathers across the room.

Raising her pan, Mrs Lambchop brought

down the omelette. 'After breakfast, what?' she said. 'A game of Monopoly?'

'Please, not again.' Arthur sighed. 'If I'd known this adventure would be so boring, I'd never have come.'

'The worst part,' Stanley said, 'is not knowing how long it will last.'

'The beginning wasn't boring,' Arthur said as they began their breakfast. 'The beginning was fun.'

The first days had in fact been tremendously exciting. They had spent many hours at the *Star Scout*'s Magnifying Window, watching the bright globe of Earth grow steadily smaller, until it seemed at last only a pale marble in the black of space. And there had been many special sights to see: the starry beauty of the Milky Way, the planets – red Mars, giant Jupiter, cloudy Venus, Saturn with its shining rings.

The third evening they appeared on TV news broadcasts on Earth. Word of their voyage had been released to the press, and all over the world people were eager to learn how this extraordinary adventure was proceeding. Standing before the spaceship's camera, the Lambchops said they felt fine, looked forward to meeting the Tyrrans, and would report

nightly while they remained in TV range.

The fourth evening they floated before the camera, demonstrating weightlessness. This was greatly appreciated on Earth, and they floated again the following day.

By the sixth evening, however, they were hard-pressed to liven their appearances. Mr Lambchop recited a baseball poem, 'Casey At The Bat'. Stanley juggled tennis balls, but the Earth audience, knowing now about weightlessness, saw the balls float when he tossed them up. Arthur did imitations of a rooster, a dog, and a man stuck in a phone booth. After this, while Mrs Lambchop was singing her college song, he went behind the plastic curtain to undress for a shower and accidentally pulled the curtain down. He was mortified, and she tried later to comfort him.

'We will be remembered, Arthur, for our time in space,' she said. 'Nobody will care about a curtain.'

'I will be remembered *forever*,' Arthur said. 'A hundred million people saw me in my underwear.'

The next day was Stanley's birthday, and just after dinner the screen lit up. There was the President in his shirtsleeves, behind his desk in Washington, D.C.

'Well, here I am working late again,' the President said. 'It's a tough job, believe me. Happy birthday, Stanley Lambchop! I've arranged a surprise. First, your friends from school.'

There was silence for a moment, broken only by the clearing of throats, and then, from all the millions of miles away, came the voices of Stanley's classmates singing, 'Happy Birthday, dear Stanley! Happy Birthday to you!'

Stanley was tremendously pleased. 'Thanks, everybody!' he said. 'You too, Mr President.'

'That was just the U.S.A. part,' said the President. 'Ready over there in London, Queen?'

'We are indeed,' the Queen's voice said cheerfully. 'And now, Master Lambchop, our famous Westminster Boys' Choir!'

From England, the beautiful voices of the famous choir sang 'Happy Birthday, Stanley!' all over again, and then other children sang it from Germany, Spain, and France.

All this attention to Stanley made Arthur jealous, and when the President said, 'By the way, Arthur, you entertained us wonderfully the other night,' he was sure this was a tease about his appearance in underwear. But he was wrong.

'Those imitations!' the President said. 'Especially the fellow in the phone booth. Darn good!'

'Indeed!' the Queen added from England. 'We were greatly amused.'

'Oh, thank you!' said Arthur, cheered. 'I –'

The screen had gone blank.

They had travelled too far. There would be no more voices from Earth, no voices but their own until they heard what the Tyrrans had to say.

'Suppose the Tyrrans have forgotten we're coming?' Stanley said. 'We might just sail around in space *forever*.'

They had finished the breakfast omelette, and were now setting out the Monopoly board because there was nothing more interesting to do.

'They don't even know our names,' Arthur said. 'What will they call us?'

'Earth people!' said a deep voice.

'Very probably,' said Mr Lambchop. ' "Earth people" seems – Who said that?'

'Not me,' said both Stanley and Arthur.

'Not *I*,' said Mrs Lambchop, correcting. 'But who –'

'Earth people!' The voice, louder now, came from the *Star Scout*'s radio. 'Greetings from the great planet Tyrra and its mighty people! Do you hear?'

'Oh, my!' Mr Lambchop turned up the volume. 'It's them!'

'*They*,' said Mrs Lambchop.

'For heaven's sake, Harriet!' Mr Lambchop said, and spoke loudly into the microphone. 'Hello, Tyrra. Earth people here. Party of four. Peace-loving family.'

'Peace-loving?' said the voice. 'Good! So is mighty Tyrra! Where are you, Earth people?'

Stanley checked his star maps. 'We're just where the tail of Ralph's Comet meets star number three million and forty-seven. Now what?'

'Right,' said the Tyrran voice. 'Keep going till you pass a star formation that looks like a foot. You can't miss it. Then, just past a lopsided little white moon, start down. You'll see a pointy mountain, then a big field. Land there. See you soon, Earth people!'

'You bet!' Mr Lambchop said, and turned to his family. 'The first contact with another planet! We are making history!'

They passed the foot-shaped star formation, then the lopsided moon, and Stanley piloted the *Star Scout* down. The darkness of space vanished as it descended, and at last the Lambchops saw clearly the planet it had taken so long to reach.

Tyrra was smallish as planets go, but nicely round and quite pretty, all in shades of brown with markings not unlike the oceans and continents of Earth. A pointy mountain came into sight, and beyond it a big field.

'There!' Stanley pressed the 'Landing' button.

Whrooom! went the *Star Scout*'s rockets. The spaceship hovered, then touched down.

Peering out, the Lambchops saw only a brown field, with tan trees at the far side and brownish hills beyond.

'Curious,' said Mr Lambchop. 'Where are –'

Suddenly a message came, but not the sort they expected.

'Surrender, Earth people!' said the radio. 'Your spaceship is trapped by our unbreakable trapping cable! You are prisoners of Tyrra! Surrender!'

CHAPTER FIVE

The Tyrrans

Unbreakable trapping cable? Prisoners? Surrender?
The Lambchops could scarcely believe their
ears.

'I don't call *that* peaceful,' said Mrs
Lambchop. 'Our President has been misled.'

'I wish we had gone to the seaside.' Mr
Lambchop shook his head. 'But *how* are we
trapped? I don't –' He pointed to the
Magnifying Window. 'What's that?'

A thin blue line, like a thread, had been
passed over the *Star Scout*. Stanley switched on
the wiper above the big window and the first
flick of its blade parted the blue line.

'Drat!' said the radio.

Other voices rose, startled, and then the deep voice spoke again. 'Earth people! We're sending a messenger! A regular, ordinary Tyrran, just to show what we're like.'

For long moments, the Lambchops kept their eyes on the tan trees across the field.

'There!' Arthur said suddenly. 'Coming toward – Oh! Oh, my . . .' His voice trailed away.

The Tyrran messenger came slowly forward to stand before the big window, a muscular, scowling young man with a curling moustache, wearing shorts and carrying a club.

The moustache was very large. The messenger was not.

'That man,' Mrs Lambchop said slowly, 'is only three inches tall.'

185

'At most,' Mr Lambchop said. 'It is a magnifying window.'

The Tyrran seemed to be calling something. Arthur opened the door a crack, and the words came clearly now. '– afraid to let us see you, Earth people? Because I'm so enormous? Hah! *All* Tyrrans are this big!'

Flinging the door wide, Arthur showed himself. 'Well, I'm a *small* Earth person!' he shouted. 'The rest are even bigger than me!'

'*I*, not me,' Mrs Lambchop said. 'And don't tease, Arth – Oh! He's fainted!'

Wetting her handkerchief with cold water, she jumped down from the *Star Scout* and ran to dab the Tyrran's tiny brow.

Cries rose again from the spaceship's radio. 'A giant killed Ik! . . . There's another, even bigger! . . . Oh, gross! . . . Look! Ik's all right!'

The Tyrran, by grasping Mrs Lambchop's handkerchief, had indeed pulled himself up. Furious, he swung his club, but managed only to tap the top of her shoe. 'Ouch! Scat!' she said, and he darted back across the field.

'Oh, my!' said the radio. 'Never mind about surrendering, Earth people! A truce committee is on the way!'

★ ★ ★

At first they saw only a tiny flag, fluttering like a white butterfly far across the brown field, but at last the Tyrran committee drew close, and the Lambchops, waiting now outside the *Star Scout*, could make each little person out.

The flag was carried by the scowling young man with the moustache and the club. The other members of the committee, a bit smaller even than he, were a red-faced man wearing a uniform with medals across the chest, a stout lady in a yellow dress and a hat with flowers on it, and two older men in blue suits, one with wavy white hair, the other thin and bald.

The committee halted, staring bravely up.

'I am General Ap!' shouted the uniformed man. 'Commander of all Tyrran forces!'

Stanley stepped forward. 'Chief Pilot Stanley Lambchop,' he said. 'From Earth. These are my parents, Mr and Mrs George Lambchop. And my brother Arthur.'

'President Ot of Tyrra, and Mrs Ot,' said General Ap, indicating the wavy-haired man and the lady. 'The bald chap is Dr Ep, our Chief Scientist. The grouchy one with the flag is my aide, Captain Ik.'

No one seemed sure what to say next. A few polite remarks were exchanged – 'Nice meeting you, Earth people!' . . . 'Such a pretty planet, Tyrra!' . . . 'Thank you. Were you very long in space?' – and Mr Lambchop realized suddenly that the Tyrrans were uncomfortable talking almost straight up. He got down on his knees, the other Lambchops following his example, and the Tyrrans at once lowered their heads in relief.

'Right!' said General Ap. 'All reasonable people here! A truce, eh?'

'I'm for war, frankly,' growled Captain Ik, but Stanley pretended not to hear. 'A truce? Good idea,' he said. 'We come in peace.'

Mrs Ot sniffed. 'Not very peaceful, frightening poor Captain Ik.' She pointed at Arthur. 'That giant shouted at him!'

'My son is not a giant,' Mrs Lambchop said. 'It's just that you Tyrrans are – how to put it? – unusually *petite*.'

'Ik's the biggest we've got, actually,' said General Ap. 'We hoped he'd scare you.'

President Ot raised his hand. 'No harm

done! Come! TyrraVille, our capital, is but a stroll away.'

The Lambchops, equipped now with handy magnifying lenses from the *Star Scout*'s science kit, followed the committee.

TyrraVille lay just across the brown field, behind the tan trees, no larger than an Earth-size tennis court.

CHAPTER SIX

Tyrra Ville

'Gosh!' Stanley said. 'It makes me homesick, in a way.'

Except for its size, and the lack of greenness, the Tyrran capital was indeed much like a small village on Earth. A Main Street bustled with Tyrrans shopping and running errands; there were handsome school and public buildings, two churches with spires as high as Mr Lambchop's waist, and side streets of pretty houses with lawns like neat brown postage stamps.

Captain Ik, still angry, marched on ahead, but the rest of the committee halted at the head of Main Street.

'We'll just show you *around*, eh?' said President Ot. 'Safer, I think.'

The Lambchops saw at once the risk of walking streets scarcely wider than their feet. Escorted by the committee, they circled the little capital, bending often to make use of their magnifying lenses. Mrs Ot took care to indicate points of particular interest, among them Ux Field, a sports centre, Admiral Ux Square, Ux Park, and the Ux Science Centre Building. ('Mrs Ot's grandfather,' whispered General Ap. 'Very rich!')

The tour caused a great stir. Everywhere the tiny citizens of TyrraVille waved from windows and rooftops. At the Science Centre, the last stop, journalists took photographs, and the Lambchops were treated to Grape Fizzola, the Tyrran national drink, hundreds of bottles of which were emptied into four tubs to make Earth-size portions.

Refreshed by his Fizzola, Arthur took a little run and hurdled a large part of TyrraVille, landing in Ux Square. 'Arthur!' Mrs Lambchop scolded, and he hurdled back.

'Aren't kids the dickens?' said a Tyrran mother, looking on. 'Mine – Stop *tugging*, Herbert!' These last words seemed addressed to the ground beside her. 'My youngest,' she explained.

Stanley squinted. 'I can hardly – He's just a *dot*.'

'Dot yourself!' said an angry voice. 'Big-a-rooney! *You're* the funny-looking one!'

'Herbert!' his mother said. 'It is rude to make fun of people for their shape or size!'

'As I said myself, often, when Stanley was flat!' Mrs Lambchop exclaimed. 'If only –'

'Surrender, Earth people!'

The cry had come from Captain Ik, who appeared now from behind the Science Centre, staggering beneath the weight of a box-like machine almost as big as he was, with a tube sticking out of it.

'Surrender!' he shouted. 'You cannot resist our Magno-Titanic Paralyser Ray! Tyrra will yet be saved!'

'There's a truce, Ik!' barked General Ap. 'You can't –'

'Yes, I can! First – Ooops!' Captain Ik's knees had buckled, but he recovered himself. 'First I'll paralyse the one who scared me back there in the field!'

Yellow light flickered up at Arthur from the Magno-Titanic Paralyser.

'Yikes!' said Arthur, as shrieks rose from the crowd.

But it was not on Arthur that the Magno-Titanic beam landed. Stanley had sprung forward to protect his brother, and the light shone now on his chest and shoulders. Mrs Lambchop almost fainted.

Suddenly her fright was gone.

Stanley was smiling. The yellow rays still flickering upon him, he rolled his head and wiggled his hands to show that he was fine. 'It's nice, actually,' he said. 'Like a massage.'

The crowd hooted. 'It only works on people Tyrran size!' someone called. 'You're a ninny, Ik!' Then Captain Ik was marched off by a Tyrran policeman, and the crowd, still laughing, drifted away.

Mrs Lambchop spoke sternly to the committee. ' "Tyrra will yet be saved?" What did Captain Ik mean? And why, pray tell, did he attempt to paralyse my son?'

The Ots and General Ap exchanged glances. Dr Ep stared at the ground.

'Ah!' said President Ot. 'Well . . . The fact is, we're having a . . . A crisis, actually. Yes. And Ik, well, he, ah –'

'Oh, tell them!' Mrs Ot burst suddenly into tears. 'About the Super-Gro! Tell, for heaven's sake!'

Puzzled, the Lambchops stared at her. The sky had darkened, and now a light rain began to fall.

'Wettish, eh?' said General Ap. 'Can't offer shelter, I'm afraid. No place large enough.'

'The *Star Scout* will do nicely,' said Mrs Lambchop. 'Let us return to it for tea.'

CHAPTER SEVEN

President Ot's Story

'Tea *does* help. I am quite myself again.' Mrs Ot nodded to her husband. 'Go on, dear. Tell.'

Rain drummed faintly on the *Star Scout*, making even cosier the scene within. About the dining-table, the Lambchops occupied their usual places. The Tyrrans sat atop the table on thumbtacks pushed down to serve as stools, sipping from tiny cups Mrs Lambchop had fashioned from aluminium foil, and nibbling crumbs of her home-made ginger snaps.

Now, sighing, President Ot set down his cup.

'You will have observed, Lambchops,' he

198

said, 'how greatly we have enjoyed these tasty refreshments. The fact is, Tyrra has for some time been totally without fresh food or water fit to drink. We live now only by what tins and bottles we had in store.'

Mrs Ot made a face. 'Pink meat spreads, and spinach. And that *dreadful* Fizzola.'

'A bit sweet, yes,' said General Ap. 'Gives one gas, too. But –'

'Never mind!' cried Mrs Ot.

President Ot continued. 'The cause of our tragedy, Lambchops, was Super-Gro. An invention of Dr Ep's. Super-Gro, Ep promised, would double our crops, make them double size, double delicious as well. A great concept, he said.'

'We scientists,' said Dr Ep, 'dream larger than other men.'

'For three days, at the Science Centre,' President Ot went on, 'Ep brewed his Super-Gro. Great smelly vats of it, enough for the whole planet. But then . . . Oh, no Tyrran will ever forget that fourth day! I myself was strolling through Ux Park. How beautiful it was! The trees and grass so green, the sky –'

'Green?' said Arthur. 'But everything's *brown* here, not green!'

'A mishap,' murmured Dr Ep. 'With the Super-Gro.'

'Mishap?' barked General Ap. 'The stuff *exploded*, Ep! All over the place!'

'Well, nobody's perfect.' Dr Ep hung his head.

'All those huge vats, Lambchops!' President Ot continued. 'Boom! One after another! Shattered windows, blew the roof off the Science Centre! No one hurt, thank goodness, but great clouds of smoke, darkening the sky! And then – such dreadful luck! – it began to rain. A *tremendous* rain, mixing with the smoke, falling all over Tyrra, into the rivers, on to every field and garden, every bit of greenery.'

Rising from his thumbtack, he paced back and forth across the table.

'When the rain stopped, there was no green. None. Just brown. Worse, Ep's tests proved that our water was undrinkable, and that nowhere on Tyrra would anything grow. I broadcast at once to the nation. "Do not despair," I said, "Tyrra will soon recover." '

'Oh, good!' Mr Lambchop said.

President Ot shook his head. 'I lied. I couldn't tell the truth, for fear of causing panic, you see. The tests showed that it would be a year at least before Tyrra was green again. And long before that we will have emptied our last tin, our last bottle of Fizzola.'

He sat down again, covering his face with his hands.

'So then we . . . We sent a message, into space. Lure some other planet's spaceship, we thought. Hold it for ransom, you see, make them send food and water. Oh, shameful! Underhanded. You will never forgive us, I know . . .'

His voice trailed away, and there was only the patter of the rain.

Close to tears, the Lambchops looked at each other, then at the little people on the table top. The Tyrrans seemed particularly tiny now, and brave, and nice.

'You poor dears!' Mrs Lambchop said. 'There was no need to *conquer* us. We would help you willingly, if we could.'

The Tyrrans seemed at first unable to believe their ears. Then, suddenly, their faces shone with joy.

'Bless you!' cried General Ap.

'Saved!' Mrs Ot clapped her hands. 'We are saved!'

'Saved . . . ?' said Mrs Lambchop.

'Of course!' said President Ot. 'Don't you see? Earth's spaceships can bring food and water till – Oh! What's wrong?'

It was Arthur who explained.

'I'm very sorry,' he said. 'But there's just the *Star Scout*. Earth hasn't *got* any other spaceships. And it would take years to build them.'

The Tyrrans gasped. 'Years . . . ?' said Dr Ep.

Stanley felt so sad he could hardly speak. 'And it's no use going for food in the *Star Scout*,' he said. 'By the time we returned from Earth, you'd all be – Well, you know.'

'Dead,' said Mrs Ot.

In the *Star Scout*, a terrible silence fell. The facts were clear. The cupboards of Tyrra would soon be empty. And then all its tiny people would starve to death.

CHAPTER EIGHT

Stanley's Good Idea

The teapot was cold now, and a last cookie crumb lay unwanted on a plate. Gloom hung like a dark cloud within the *Star Scout*.

'It's not fair,' Arthur said for the third time. 'It's just not.'

'Stop saying that,' Stanley told him. 'That's four times now.'

'Five,' said Dr Ep.

General Ap tried to be cheerful. 'Ah, well . . . Still some tinned meat, eh? And plenty of Grape Fizzola. Much to be thankful for.'

'I will *never* be thankful for Grape Fizzola,' said Mrs Ot.

204

'It's just that . . .' Arthur sighed. 'I mean, Earth has so *much* food. Millions of people, and there's mostly still enough.'

The Tyrrans seemed amazed. 'Millions? You're joking?' said President Ot.

'Hah!' said General Ap. 'Dreadful crush, I should think. Millions?'

Mrs Lambchop smiled. 'With all our great nations, many millions. And still the numbers grow.'

'Well, here too.' President Ot shook his head. 'Youthful marriages, babies one after another. But *millions*? Our population – there's just TyrraVille, of course – is six hundred and eighty-three.'

'Eighty-four,' said Mrs Ot. 'Mrs Ix had a baby last night.'

Now it was the Lambchops who were amazed.

'Just TyrraVille?' Arthur cried. 'But TyrraVille's your *capital*, you said!'

'Well, it would have to be, wouldn't it, dear?' said Mrs Ot.

Stanley shook his head. 'On the whole planet, only six hundred and eighty-four Tyrrans! Gosh, I'll bet – Wait!'

An idea had come to him. Stanley had had exciting ideas before, but none that excited him as this one did.

'Mrs Ot!' he shouted. 'How much do you weigh?'

'Stanley!' said Mrs Lambchop.

Mrs Ot was not offended. 'Actually, I've

slimmed a bit. Though not, sadly, in the hips. I'm six ounces, young man. Why do you ask?'

The words rushed out of Stanley. 'Because if you're average only children would be even lighter, then all the Tyrrans put together would weigh – Let me figure this out!'

'Less than three hundred pounds,' said Mr Lambchop, who was good at maths. 'Though I don't see –' Then he did see. 'Oh! Good for you, Stanley!'

'The lad's bright, we know,' said General Ap. 'But what –'

'General!' said Mr Lambchop. 'Summon all Tyrrans here to the *Star Scout*! Fetch what remains of your tinned food and Grape Fizzola! Perhaps Earth can be your home till Tyrra is green again!'

CHAPTER NINE

The Weighing

From each little house on each little street, the Tyrrans came, every man, woman, and child, even Captain Ik with a guard from the jail. The rain had stopped, and the evening light shone gold on the brown field in which the tiny people stood assembled.

President Ot addressed them. 'Fellow Tyrrans! I must confess that your government has deceived you! The truth is: It will be at least a year before our fields and streams are fit again.'

Cries rose from the crowd. 'We were lied to! . . . Lordy, talk about bad news! . . . We'll starve! . . . Shoot the scientists!'

'Wait!' shouted President Ot. 'We are offered refuge on Earth, if the voyage is possible! Pay attention, please!'

Stepping forward, Mr Lambchop read aloud from the booklet that had come with the *Star Scout*.

' "Your spacecraft has been designed for safety as well as comfort. Use only as directed." ' He raised his voice. ' "Do not add weight by bringing souvenirs aboard *or by inviting friends to ride with you*." '

Cries rose again. 'That did it! . . . We're not *souvenirs*! . . . He said no friends either, stupid! . . . We've had it, looks like!'

Mr Lambchop raised his hand. 'There is still hope! But you must all be weighed! Also the supplies you would require for the trip!'

The *Star Scout*'s bathroom scales, set down in the field, proved too high for the Tyrrans, and the weighing was briefly delayed until Arthur, using the Monopoly board, made a ramp by which they could easily mount.

General Ap barked orders. 'Right, then! Groups of twenty to twenty-five, families together! And don't jiggle!'

The Ots and six other families marched up on to the scale, beside which Mrs Lambchop stood with pad and pencil. 'Seven and one-quarter pounds!' she said, writing it down.

'Next!' shouted General Ap, but the Ot group was already starting down, and another marching up.

Group after group mounted the scale. There *was* jiggling, due to excited children, but Mrs Lambchop took care to wait until the needle was still. Within an hour the entire population of Tyrra had been weighed, along with its supplies of tinned food and Fizzola, and she added up.

'Tyrrans, two hundred and thirty-nine,' she announced. 'Food and Fizzola, one hundred and forty. Total: Three hundred and seventy-nine pounds!'

'Are we saved? Or are we too fat?' came a cry.

'Too soon to tell!' Mr Lambchop called back. 'We must see how we can lighten our ship!'

A good start was made by discarding the *Star Scout*'s dining-table and one steel bunk,

since Stanley and Arthur could easily share.
Then out went Stanley's tennis balls, extra
sweater, and his Chief Pilot zip jacket with the
American flag; out went Arthur's knee socks,
raincoat, and a plastic gorilla he had smuggled
aboard. Mr and Mrs Lambchop added their
extra clothing, lamps, kitchenware, the
Monopoly game, and at last, the posters of
Mexico and France.

The crowd stood hushed as the pile was
weighed. Somewhere a baby cried, and its
parents scolded it.

'Three hundred and seventy-seven pounds!'
Mrs Lambchop announced. 'Oh, dear!' she

whispered to President Ot. 'Two less than we need.'

'I see.' President Ot, after a moment's thought, climbed up on to the scale. 'Good news, Tyrrans!' he called. 'Almost all of us are saved!'

Cheers went up, and then someone shouted, 'What do you mean, *almost* all?'

'We weigh, as a nation, a bit too much,' President Ot explained. 'But only four, if largish, need stay behind. I shall be one. Will three more volunteer?'

Murmurs rose from the crowd. 'That's *my* kind of President! . . . Leave Ik behind! . . . How about you, Ralph? . . . Ask somebody else, darn you!'

The matter was quickly resolved. 'I won't go without you, dear,' Mrs Ot told her husband, and Captain Ik, hoping to regain popularity, announced that he too would remain.

General Ap was the fourth volunteer. 'Just an old soldier, ma'am,' he told Mrs Lambchop. 'Lived a full life, time now to just fade away, to –'

'Hey! Wait!'

Arthur was pointing to the scale.

'We forgot *that*,' he said. 'We can leave the scale behind. Now nobody has to stay!'

CHAPTER TEN

Heading Home

'Mr and Mrs Ix, and the new baby?' said President Ot, beside his wife on a ledge above the Magnifying Window. 'Ah, yes, on the fridge!'

The people of Tyrra were being made as comfortable as possible in the various nooks and crannies of the *Star Scout*. Stanley and Arthur had cleared a cupboard where Tyrra High School students could study during the trip, and Mrs Lambchop had cut up sheets to make hundreds of little blankets, and put out bits of cotton for pillows. 'Makeshift, Mrs Ix,' she said now, settling the Ixes on the fridge. 'But *such* short notice. Back a bit from the

214

edge, yes?'

'Short notice indeed,' said Mrs Ix. 'So many –'

'Not to worry.' Mrs Lambchop smiled proudly. 'My son, the Chief Pilot, will call ahead.'

From a nearby shelf, Captain Ik whispered an apology for attempting to paralyse Arthur. 'Between you and I, I didn't really think it would work,' he said.

'Between you and *me*,' said Mrs Lambchop. 'But thank you, Captain Ik.' She turned to Stanley. 'We're all ready, dear!'

Stanley checked his controls. 'Let's go!'

'Tyrrans!' President Ot called for attention. 'Our national anthem!'

Everywhere in the *Star Scout*, Tyrrans rose, their right hands over their hearts. '*Hmmmm . . .*' hummed Mrs Ot, setting a key, and they began to sing.

'Tyrra, the lovely! Tyrra, the free!
Hear, dear planet, our promise to thee!
Where e'er we may go, where e'er we may roam,
We'll come back to Tyrra, Tyrra our home!'

The words echoed in the softly lit cabin. Many Tyrrans were weeping, and the eyes of the Lambchops, as they took their seats, glistened too.

'Be it ever so humble, there's no planet so dear,

We'll always love Tyrra, from far or from –'

Stanley pressed the 'Start' button, and – *Whroooom!* – the *Star Scout*'s rockets roared to life.

The singing stopped suddenly, and Mrs Ix cried out from the fridge. 'Oh, my! Is this thing safe?'

'Yes indeed,' Mrs Lambchop called back.

'Perhaps,' said Mrs Ix. 'But it is my belief that if Tyrrans were meant to fly, we'd have wings.'

Whroooom! Whroooom!

The *Star Scout* lifted now, gaining speed as it rose. Its mission was done. The strangers who had called from a distant planet were no longer strangers, but friends.

It was all very satisfactory, Stanley thought. The other Lambchops thought so too.

CHAPTER ELEVEN

Earth Again

'. . . real pleasure to welcome you, Tyrrans,' said the President, almost done with his speech. 'I wish you a fine year on Earth!'

Before him on the White House lawn, with newspaper and TV reporters all about, sat the Lambchops and, in a tiny grandstand built especially for the occasion, the people of Tyrra.

The Tyrrans were now applauding politely, but they looked nervous, and Mrs Lambchop guessed why. That crowd at the Space Centre for the *Star Scout*'s landing, that drive through crowded streets into Washington, D.C! Poor Tyrrans! Everywhere they looked, giant

218

buildings, giant people. How could they feel comfortable here?

But a surprise was in store. Across the lawn, a great white sheet had been spread. Now, at the President's signal, workmen pulled the sheet away.

'Welcome,' said the President, 'to TyrraVille Two!'

Gasps rose from the Tyrrans, then shouts of joy.

Before them, on what had been the White House tennis court, lay an entire village of tiny houses, one for each Tyrran family, with shops and schools and churches, and a miniature railway serving all principal streets. Begun when Stanley called ahead from space, TyrraVille Two had been completed well before the *Star Scout*'s arrival, thanks to rush deliveries from leading toy stores in Washington and New York.

The excited Tyrrans ran from the grandstand to explore their new homes, and soon happy voices rose from every window and doorway of TyrraVille Two. 'Nice furniture! . . . Hooray! Fresh lemonade! No more Fizzola! . . . In the cupboards, see? Shirts, dresses, suits, shoes! . . . Underwear, even!'

The Ots, General Ap, Dr Ep, and Captain Ik

came back to say goodbye, and the Lambchops knelt to touch fingertips in farewell. The TV men filmed this, and Arthur made everyone laugh, pretending to be paralysed by the touch of Captain Ik. Then the newsmen left, the Tyrrans returned to TyrraVille Two, and only the President remained with the Lambchops on the White House lawn.

'Well, back to work.' The President sighed. 'Goodbye, Lambchops. You're all heroes, you know. Saved the nation.'

'Not really,' Stanley said. 'They couldn't have conquered us.'

'Well, you know what I mean,' the President said. 'You folks care to stay for supper?'

'Thank you, no,' Mrs Lambchop said. 'It is quite late, and this has been an exciting but very tiring day.'

It was bedtime when they got home. Stanley and Arthur had a light supper, with hot chocolate to help them sleep, after which Mr and Mrs Lambchop tucked them in and said goodnight.

The brothers lay quietly in the darkness for a moment. Then Arthur chuckled.

'The Magno–Titanic Paralyser *was* sort of scary,' he said. 'You were brave, Stanley, protecting me.'

'That's okay,' Stanley said. 'You're my brother, right?'

'I know . . .' Arthur was sleepy now. 'Stanley? When the Tyrrans go back, will their land and water be okay? Will they let us know?'

'I guess so.' Stanley was drowsy too. 'Goodnight, Arthur.'

'Goodnight,' said Arthur, and soon they were both asleep.

And in time, from the great farness of space, but a farness no longer strange or unknown, another message came.

'We are home. All is well.'

And again.

'We are home! Thank you, Earth! All is well!'

THE END

First published in Great Britain as three separate volumes:

Flat Stanley
First published in Great Britain 1968 by Methuen & Co Ltd
Published 1989 by Mammoth
Text copyright © 1964 Jeff Brown
Illustrations copyright © 1964 Tomi Ungerer

Stanley and the Magic Lamp
First published in Great Britain 1985 by Methuen Children's Books
as *A Lamp for the Lambchops*
Published 1989 by Mammoth
Text copyright © 1983 Jeff Brown
Illustrations copyright © 1985 Quentin Blake

Stanley in Space
First published in Great Britain 1990 by Methuen Children's Books
Published 1991 by Mammoth
Text copyright © 1990 Jeff Brown
Illustrations copyright © 1990 Philippe Dupasquier

This edition first published 1992 by Dean
Paperback edition published 1993 by Mammoth
an imprint of Egmont Children's Books Ltd
Michelin House, 81 Fulham Road, London SW3 6RB

Reprinted 1994, 1995, 1996, 1998

ISBN 0 7497 1483 2

A CIP catalogue record for this title
is available from the British Library

Printed and bound in Great Britain
by Cox & Wyman Ltd, Reading, Berkshire